The
Black Phantom
of Ravenhurst

Willem G. Vandehulst

The
Black Phantom
of Ravenhurst

PAIDEIA PRESS
Jordan Station, Ontario, Canada

First published in Dutch as *Zwarte kraaien*, © Willem G. Vandehulst Jr.
Cover painting and illustrations by Willem G. Vandehulst Jr.

ISBN 0-88815-547-6
Printed in Canada.

HROUGH the woods rode a solitary horseman. The woods were stark black on white—black trees and white snow. The rider was laboriously picking his way through a dense stand of tree trunks. His horse's legs sank deep into the snow, now and then stumbling over hidden roots.

The rider patted his mount's neck. "Come on, Oscar, lift those hooves a little higher. It won't be long now and you'll be able to rest in a warm stable."

The words were meant to encourage the horse, but they carried an undertone of uneasiness. The rider squinted ahead through the maze of tree trunks. When was he going to see daylight? These woods seemed to keep getting denser and darker. He ducked to avoid a low branch. Too late. The branch struck his shoulder, springing loose a shower of snow. Ice-water trickled down his neck. He knocked the snow off his collar and dug a chunk of rye bread from his saddlebag. His hand groped under his fur cloak near his hip. Then he remembered that he had lost his knife yesterday and a dark scowl passed over his face.

5

Breaking off a large piece of the bread, he bent forward to feed it to the horse. The horse's long velvet lips reached eagerly for it. Then the rider broke off a piece for himself and chewed thoughtfully as his eyes scoured the surrounding woods. He was afraid that he was lost. He should have reached the old hessian road long ago.

Again he patted the horse's neck, not so much to encourage the horse as himself. Yes, he had to admit it: he was worried. The light of day was fading; whites and blacks were merging into murky gray. Would he be able to reach the village before dark?

"Come on, Oscar, let's pick up the pace a little. You're getting tired, aren't you boy? And hungry. Well, so am I. But it shouldn't be long now."

This should have been the last day of a four-day journey which had taken him through swamps and forests and over hills. According to his calculations, he should have reached his destination this afternoon. This morning he had left his inn before daylight; the innkeeper had held the lantern while he had saddled his horse. Now, after riding all day, he saw no trace of a road or dwellings. There was nothing but the stillness of the forest.

Suddenly a hoarse bellow broke the stillness. A snow-caked bush exploded, and the rider's way was blocked by a wild boar ready to charge. Its dark flanks trembled and the bristly black hair on its spine rose. Snorting another gutteral challenge, the boar brandished its yellow tusks.

The rider didn't scare easily. Even as his hand shot to the sword hanging from his belt, he asked himself whether it was the best defense against this angry beast.

The horse, however, panicked. With a piercing whinny, he reared up high, lashing wildly with its forelegs. The rider fought for his balance for a moment, but then slid sideways from the saddle and tumbled into the snow. The commotion frightened the wild boar. With a hoarse squeal, it swerved into the trees, and disappeared in the thick undergrowth.

The rider climbed to his feet and beat the snow from his cloak. He was angry with himself. Even under the most trying conditions he had never before fallen off his horse, and now he suddenly found himself dumped in the snow. But looking over at his mount, he saw why he had fallen. When the horse had reared, throwing the full weight of the rider against the saddle, the cinch had broken and the saddle had been tossed into the snow.

The rider scowled. Now he would have to walk. That wouldn't be easy in this deep snow which concealed treacherous roots and fallen branches. He stooped, picked up the saddle and tossed it back onto the horse. Then he took the horse by the reins and started plodding through the woods, his boots sinking into the snow. Slowly the shadows in the forest deepened.

After struggling along for some time, the man stopped to look about. The trees seemed more widely spaced here. Yes, that had to be the old hessian road ahead. At last! If he followed this road, which skirted the woods, he should soon come to a village.

With new heart he trudged on through the stillness. Then, abruptly, he stopped. He had heard a faint noise. After a few moments, he heard it again, clearer this time. Coming up behind him, it sounded like the crunch of wagon wheels on snow. The man turned to look back down the road. The road carved a white swath through the woods. Two black work horses lumbered into sight around a curve in the road. They were pulling a wagon loaded with branches.

The driver was turned about in the seat to rearrange the branches. The weary traveler moved to the side of the road to wait for the wagon. Perhaps he could borrow a knife from the wagon driver to fix the cinch on his saddle. Why had he been stupid enough to lose his own knife?

Again he looked back. Strange! The driver was now leaning back against the load of branches. His head, cradled by his deep collar, hung forward on his chest as if he were dozing. "That is odd," he thought. "Only a moment ago the man was straightening his load. Or did my eyes deceive me?"

The wagon was almost on him, and the driver still seemed to be dozing.

"Hey, driver! May I borrow your knife?"

The driver started, as if waking from a sleep. "Eh? What's that? . . . Who are you?"

As he reined in his horses, the wagon creaked to a halt.

The horseman, a wealthy merchant, felt himself growing angry. He was not used to being spoken to so impolitely, and certainly not by a mere farmer. He hid his irritation, however.

"May I please borrow your knife? My cinch broke."

The driver eyed him dourly from beneath bushy eyebrows, but he did produce a knife from beneath his bulky coat.

"Here," he grunted. "But hurry up. I don't have all day."

Were his eyes deceiving him again, or did he see the branches on the wagon move? As he took the knife from the driver, he once more glanced at the load of branches. Then he took hold of the cinch and punched some extra holes in it, making one end a little longer. What a fine, sharp knife! In fact, it was very unusual for a poor farmer to have such a knife. The blade was made of the finest steel and the ivory handle was carved into the shape of a raven.

"A fine knife. What does the raven stand for? You wouldn't consider selling it, would you? I could use a good knife."

The driver spat into the snow. "It's not for sale. And if you're done with it, I'll have it back now."

The wagon was moving even before the traveler handed the knife back. Seething, he watched the farmer drive away. What a rude, cranky fellow! Why was he in such a hurry?

But look! The branches seemed to move again. Wasn't something sticking out of the load? The wagon was some distance away already and the light was poor, so he couldn't be sure. But it had looked like a boot.

Puzzling over what he had seen, the traveler finished fixing his cinch and then fastened the saddle on the horse's back. Swinging up into the saddle, he continued on his way.

When he reached the end of the forest, he reined in. Gray snow clouds were massed on the far horizon, but above him a single star twinkled in a clear, dark sky. In the distance were huddled the small houses of the village he had been looking for. With their snowy roofs, they looked like a flock of sheep bedded down for the coming night. Here and there a lantern light gleamed in the gathering dusk.

To the left, the land sloped from the edge of the woods to a large marsh. Beyond the marsh lay the water of a wide river, a dull silver line in the dark gray landscape.

Look—how strange!—the wagon was turning toward that spooky world of dead reeds and alder thickets. Why didn't the driver take his load to the village? Why was he heading into that vast swampland so near to nightfall?

The rider shrugged his shoulders. It was none of his business. Once more he puzzled over the boot he thought he had seen among the branches. Had it really been a boot? He shook his head. He was tired. His eyes must have been playing tricks on him.

He spurred his horse forward, heading toward the village. As he crossed the dark field, he urged his mount into a gallop. The horse's hooves flung up chunks of snow.

Once again the rider patted his horse's neck, trying to put what he had seen out of his mind. None of it made any sense.

T'S AN outrage—that's what it is—an outrage!"

Big-bellied Thune lifted a thick arm from his coarse woollen jacket, tilted his head, and poured the contents of the stein down his throat.

"It's a crime!"

His usually gentle eyes blazed around at the circle of silent men. They were sitting in the local inn at a wooden table that had been scrubbed white. The oil lamp cast a yellow glow on the glum gathering. This group of farmers had gathered here from miles around.

Actually they were part-time farmers and part-time hunters; in the summer they tilled the land and in the winter they hunted in the vast forests. Some of their winter profit in furs had to be set aside along with a certain share of the grain harvest in order to pay the ageing countess rent for her land. The rest of the furs were used to barter with traveling peddlers for basic necessities. Most of the things the farmers bought were paid for by barter, that is, they traded their goods for goods they could not produce themselves. They led a simple but secure life. But now . . . ?

12

Suddenly they faced hard times. Soldiers from the castle had ridden from farm to farm to tell the farmers that this year the countess had tripled their rent. This meant poverty for the farmers. And hunger.

"It's an outrage!"

The men sitting near the huge fireplace turned their leathery faces to Thune, and their eyes were dark with deep anxiety.

Suddenly someone rapped hard at the inn door. The latch clinked, the door swung open, and in the doorway stood a young rider. Over his left shoulder gleamed the eyes of a tall black horse. The farmers didn't recognize the man, but by his dress and the ornate scabbard of his sword, they could tell that he was rich.

The innkeeper, who had also been sitting at the fire, stepped forward. He was a little unsure of what to do because strangers seldom stopped at his inn. Bowing deeply, he said, "Welcome, sir. Welcome to my inn."

"Thank you, innkeeper," replied the young gentleman. "Have you a bed for me and a warm stall for my horse?"

The innkeeper wrung his hands and, twisting his lip, blew aside the tassle of his night cap, which had flopped forward over his face. "I-I'm sorry, sir, but I don't have any extra beds."

"What's this? An inn without beds for guests?"

"Well . . . you see, even my own boys are sleeping in the stable. The soldiers from the castle took all my beds for themselves."

The gentleman's eyebrows rose. "That's a fine how-dee-do! Well, I guess I'd better sleep in the straw tonight too."

Then Thune stood up. "I won't hear of that. A gentleman can't sleep in the stable!"

The innkeeper stepped aside, once again swinging back the tassle of his cap.

"I have a better idea," Thune went on, "I live alone in a cabin at the edge of the woods and I have an extra bed. I'd be honored to have you as my guest. That is, if you wish—"

"Thank you, my good man. I'd be delighted to accept your offer. My name is Peter of Bettelburg. My father is called the Great Merchant of the South. And what is your name?"

"Thune, sir." He spread his two huge hands on his belly. "They call me Tubby Thune."

Peter grinned and nodded. "Yes, I see why."

One of the innkeeper's sons came forward and took the black horse's reins to lead it to the stable. The farmers looked on in silence as Peter sat down near the fireplace and helped himself to some of the partridge roasting over the fire. Slowly, however, anxiety won out over curiosity. Quietly they returned to their discussion.

At first Peter paid no attention, but suddenly, as he overheard a few words, his ears pricked up. The farmers were complaining about an impossible rent and about strange soldiers that recently had been quartered in the castle. Peter had made his long journey in order to see the Countess of Ravenhurst, and now he heard her name mentioned. He went on eating and pretended not to be listening, but he kept his ears tuned to every word.

He didn't understand much of what was being said, but it was obvious that the farmers were deeply worried. Worried and angry. Thune, who was sitting with his back toward him, gestured angrily with his powerful arms. The farmers leaned forward over the table, whispering urgently. Now it sounded as though they were talking about a mill.

Peter thought, "When I have Thune to myself, I'll have to pump him a little. Maybe he'll tell me what it's all about."

The moon stood high among the silver lined clouds. Through the quiet, snow-bright night walked two men, one of them leading a horse. A lantern hung from the saddle. They were crossing an open field surrounded by the black shadows of forest. Above the forest rose the dark silhouette of a castle with menacing peaked towers. Fearfully Thune peered from behind his upturned collar into the dark woods on their right.

For about the tenth time since they had left the inn, Peter looked up at the sky. Suddenly he stopped. "Say, Thune, old man, where are you taking me? We've been walking for over half an hour, and unless the stars mislead me, we've traveled in a huge semi-circle around those woods. Just where is your cabin?"

Thune's eyes flitted about fearfully. "In that direction, sir."

Peter was sure the big man wasn't telling the truth. Why was he misleading him? Then he noticed the fear in his eyes. What was he afraid of?

Risking a sudden guess, he said with more confidence than he felt: "Thune, your house isn't over there. It's over there—behind those woods."

"Yes, sir, but—but—"

"Why didn't we take the most direct path—straight through those woods?"

Thune shuddered, swallowed twice and then stammered, "B-b-but sir! That—that's d-d-dangerous! The mill—i-i-it's haunted!"

"Haunted? You mean by ghosts?"

"Every night there's the awfullest groaning and crying at the old mill."

Peter laughed. "Come on. You've let someone scare you with ghost stories. Tell me, did you ever see any ghosts yourself?"

"Yes, sir, I did. Honest! I saw it with my own eyes. It was wearing a black cloak and it didn't have a face. Just two glowing eyes."

When Peter saw that the good fellow was indeed terrified, he began to feel sorry for him. "Well, let's go on. And, if it bothers you, we won't go through the woods. When we get to your place, you'll have to tell me more. But if we stand here any longer, we'll freeze. Let's go."

After walking for another half hour, they reached Thune's cabin. It stood close to the edge of the woods. Peter stabled his horse in the small lean-to attached to the house and filled the feed-box with some of the fresh hay stacked in one corner of a nearby shed.

When he stepped back outside, he saw Thune checking the shutters to make sure that they were tightly fastened. Every now and then he cast frightened glances over his shoulder at the dark woods.

Soon after, in the small room lit by the weak glow of one candle, Thune was telling his story. Peter sat motionless with his back against the stones of the fireplace, letting the bulky farmer talk on without interruption. The fire in the fireplace dwindled to a mere pile of glowing ash, but Peter didn't notice.

It was a strange story. The mill in the woods was an ancient ruin. It belonged to Ravenhurst Castle, but it hadn't been used for many years. Long, long ago the castle had been occupied by Count Ravenhurst, the great-grandfather of the countess who now lived in the castle. He had been a strange and solitary man. As a matter of fact, he had been ill—mentally ill. In his diseased mind, he was sure that he was surrounded by unearthly powers which were out to get him. Wherever he went, he felt they were watching him, waiting to trap him or kill him. Bent double, he would steal down the long passages of the castle, avoiding every dark corner and niche, expecting something to leap out at him at any moment.

His sickness grew worse and worse until at last he no longer trusted anyone. Even the armed servants, with whom he surrounded himself for protection from his imaginary enemies, frightened him. For days he would lock himself in the main hall. Or sometimes he would roam about in the deep woods, staying away for weeks at a time. No one would know where he was.

Late one night—a winter night just like tonight, with snow glistening in the moonlight—two farmers passing the mill found the old man. He was hanging head down from the waterwheel of the mill, and blood was still dripping from a deep cut on his forehead.

The two farmers fetched the watchmen from the castle and left the scene, but there the stories began. One person after another ventured guesses and voiced fears. One ghastly story after another made the rounds, all of them centered on the old mill. During the long winter nights the farmers told these stories to one another until they saw ghosts hovering in the shadows, and the ancient ruin in the forest became known as the haunted mill.

The farmers who first told these stories had long since died. Now their grandchildren and great-grandchildren sat around the fire telling stories. And the story of the strange count and his mysterious death still survived. Now, however, the story wasn't told just for thrills and entertainment on cold winter nights when everyone was gathered around the warmth of the fireplace and shadows leaped high on the walls. Now, whenever people spoke of Ravenhurst Mill and the mad count, they spoke in whispers. The men glanced fearfully over their shoulders and the women carefully closed all the shutters. They seemed afraid that someone might overhear them.

What had made everyone so afraid?

ETER lay on the narrow bed in the low attic of Thune's cabin. Downstairs Thune was getting ready for bed. The squeal of hinges and the creaks of bolts sounded clearly through the floorboards. Peter smiled to himself. That huge man was scared to death of ghosts. Nevertheless, he was a good man.

The light of the candle that Thune carried with him as he moved about the house filtered through the cracks between the floorboards. At last a soft creaking sound told Peter that Thune had climbed into bed. The glimmer of the candle vanished.

Now it was quiet in the cabin. Peter lay in the dark with his hands clasped beneath his head. Despite his exhausting day, he could not fall asleep. He stared at the window, a small, gray rectangle in the darkness. But he didn't really see the window. He saw a wagon coming around a bend of a forest road. The driver was turned around on his seat to rearrange the load of branches. But then suddenly the man was facing forward, rocking from side to side as he dozed. How could he have fallen asleep so quickly?

19

More images thrust themselves before him. Now the wagon was creaking away from him and something was moving in the back among the branches. Was that a boot jutting out of the load?

Peter's eyelids grew heavy and then closed. But the images pursued him. Suddenly there were many faces, tough, weathered faces with grim lips—the farmers from the inn. Their eyes were troubled and anxious. Thune was among them, looking more frightened than anyone else.

All of a sudden the big man was standing outside in the snow and the bright moonlight. He was trying to say something, but he was so frightened that the words wouldn't come out. Trembling, he finally forced out a few words in a hoarse whisper: "L-listen—i-i-it's the g-g-ghost!"

Peter's eyes opened. Had he fallen asleep; was he dreaming? Or had he really heard a voice calling his name? He strained to listen.

Nothing. It was absolutely still in the cabin. Suddenly, however, a sound reached his ears. That must be what he had heard a moment ago in his sleep. Thune's voice came from below through the cracks of the floorboards. Moaning in terror, he was trying to call his upstairs guest, but he was afraid to call out loud. His voice was a hoarse whisper.

"Master Peter! Master Peter! Th-the ghost—d-d-do you hear it? It's at the mill."

Peter sat bolt upright in bed. Sure enough, now he heard it too. Straining forward, he listened attentively. Yes, now he could tell that it was coming from the woods. What was it? What could be making that noise in the middle of the night?

Peter shuddered. Thune had called it groaning, but it sounded more like wailing, now and then broken by a piercing howl. Momentarily Peter thought of a wolf or a wounded boar. But no; this sound was more terrifying.

Now it was still again, though he waited, sitting upright in bed. The blood-chilling sound echoed on in his ears, but all remained still. He stirred angrily under the blankets. If he were a real man, he'd saddle his horse and ride out to investigate.

"D-d-did you hear the ghost, s-s-sir?" Thune hissed from below.

Peter was becoming disgusted with the cowering man downstairs. He hung his head over the edge of the bed and whispered down, "Ah, man, quit your blubbering!"

Then he became even angrier, but at himself this time. Why was he whispering? Was he afraid to talk out loud? A fine example he set! With a quick leap he was standing beside his bed, groping for his clothes. Afraid of a ghost? Never!

Quickly he clambered down the old ladder. From the bed in the corner of the cabin came a smothered moan: "O-o-oh!" Thune had been reduced to a quivering mass of fear buried deep under his bedclothes.

Peter slid back the door bolts and stepped out into the bright night. He took his horse from the shed and saddled it. Then he swung onto his back and, patting him on the neck, said, "Let's go, Oscar. Attaboy!"

At a brisk gallop he dashed across the field of snow toward the dark shadow of the forest. The last few meters he reined in his horse a little, intending to approach the first trees cautiously. Perhaps resolve tempered with caution could pierce the solid black shadows which waited threateningly beyond the gray trunks. In his mind he still heard the last echoes of the horrible wailing that had come from this direction, and he was almost sorry he had decided to investigate. Why hadn't he stayed in the cozy warmth of his bed? Tomorrow morning would have been a much better time to do some investigating. In this darkness he couldn't see anything anyway.

He shrugged his shoulders and kept looking for an opening into the woods. Dense undergrowth between the trees kept blocking his way. The horse plunged forward into the darkness as Peter slowly and carefully picked his way through the trees. Oscar's footing was constantly threatened by treacherous roots and vines which lay like traps under the snow.

Suddenly Peter drew the reins taut and listened intently. From nearby came a soft rushing sound—the sound of running water. He nodded. The mill had to be located on a river or stream.

He urged his horse on again. A few moments later he found himself riding along a stream. All he had to do now was follow it until he came to the mill. Huge boulders, however, soon forced him to make wide detours away from the stream.

At last Peter spotted a gap in the woods ahead. He rode toward a moonlit space cleared of all trees, and there stood the old mill. Hanging back in the shadows of the trees, he stopped and looked. At first sight the mill looked something like an old barn. But it was too tall and narrow to be a barn. The stream ran past the rear of the building, where out of the wall jutted a huge water wheel on a thick wooden axle.

A crudely crafted sluice had at one time channeled the water over the top of the water wheel. This powered the wheel to turn the grinding stone inside the mill. Over the years, however, part of the sluice had collapsed, and the water no longer reached the wheel. It cascaded back into the stream several meters away from its goal.

Oscar nervously tossed his head, turning his ears forward, backward, and then forward again. His keen senses seemed to have picked up something. But Peter heard nothing but the quiet gurgle of the water.

He patted Oscar's neck. "Easy, boy. What's the matter?"

The horse remained restless, but Peter ignored him. Studying the mill, he saw that it had two stories. Directly above the main door, which was standing ajar, was a large opening, and on either side of the opening was a window. In the moonlight, the mill with its sloping, snow-covered roof and its two gaping black windows looked like a giant, eyeless skull.

Carefully Peter slid out of the saddle. Tying Oscar's reins to a nearby branch, he cautiously looked around, thinking. Had the wailing sound that he'd heard from Thune's attic really come from this ancient mill? It hardly seemed likely. Those ghost stories told by the local farmers were the products of superstitious, frightened minds. Still . . . he had heard the sound too. Peter rubbed his chin. Maybe it really had been a wolf or a wounded boar . . .

Now he was feeling the same unpleasant crawling sensation along his spine that he had felt in the attic. It was the first stage of a cold fear that threatened to overpower him. He knew very well that he had heard no wolf

or boar. Angrily he shook off his creeping fear. Throwing back his shoulders, he walked with long, firm strides across the moonlit clearing to the door of the mill.

Here he stopped and looked about, smiling at his own uneasiness. It was easy to see that no one had been here recently. Not even an animal. The only footprints in the snow were his own.

He walked around to the other side of the mill. Here, too, the snow was undisturbed. No one could have come to the mill before him. Returning to the front of the mill, he pushed the door open wider. Now, spurred on by curiosity, he stepped inside.

His eyes adjusted slowly to the darkness. Moonlight fell through cracks in the plank wall and traced pale lines across the mud floor and the broken millstone worn smooth and hollow. A shaky ladder with two missing rungs led up to an opening in the ceiling.

He started forward and then suddenly jerked back in fright. His foot had struck something soft. Stooping, he saw that he'd bumped into a stack of mildewed grain sacks. Cautiously he went on, looking the place over very closely, but he noticed nothing unusual. In the rear wall where the axle jutted outside there seemed to be a couple of loose boards. He stepped toward the place and again he flinched back. Brrr! Cobwebs! He wiped the sticky threads from his face.

He pulled one of the loose boards aside and put his head out through the opening. Down below, the swirling water of the stream rushed by, splashing over the stones that lay in the creek like tiny islands. The water wheel was almost within his reach.

Long ago on a night such as this, two farmers had found the body of the old count dangling from this wheel. Peter felt irritated at the stupid people who had turned the event into a ghost story. But he felt even more irritated with himself. Why was he standing here in this cold, abandoned mill in the middle of the night when he could be lying in a warm bed getting some badly needed sleep? He had to be rested and fresh in the morning for his visit with the countess. He'd better get back to the cabin and to his bed in the attic.

He turned to walk back to his horse.

Then for a split second he stood rooted to the spot. Suddenly, however, he was moving: dodging quick as a cat. Just in time! In a beam behind his head quivered the handle of a knife, the blade buried deep in the wood. He could still hear the twang of the vibrating weapon. It had skimmed past his ear with the swiftness of an arrow.

Again he looked at the open door to confirm what he had seen. A glimpse was all he had gotten, but it had been enough. A tall, broad figure had been standing in the doorway. It had been wearing a wide cloak and a broad-rimmed hat. Most striking, however, had been the face: black, with no features but two pale, piercing eyes.

It had stood there motionless—a dark phantom. Then suddenly a black hand had appeared from beneath the cloak, and between the fingers of that hand had been the steel edge of a knife blade. Moonlight flashing on the bright metal had saved his life. But when he had turned from glancing at the quivering knife, the black figure had vanished as soundlessly as it had come.

With a quick tug Peter pulled the knife out of the

beam near his shoulder and sprang toward the door, determined to chase down his ambusher. He felt no fear; he thought only about catching the man. When he reached the doorway, however, he halted, shocked. The man had vanished, and the only footprints in the snow were those made by his own boots.

Who could flee across the snow without leaving footprints? No one. Only a ghost.

In his hand, however, he felt the dead weight of the knife. That was no ghost knife. It was real. He held it up in the moonlight and examined it as if to reassure himself. But his breath caught in his throat. It was a well-made steel knife with a white ivory handle. And carved into the handle was the shape of a black bird—a raven!

HE next morning a blue, cloudless sky stretched over the woods, and the white fields glared brightly in the cold winter sunlight. Thune stood at the door of his cabin to say goodbye to his guest. Peter, who had already mounted his horse, bent forward toward his host.

"For your hospitality," he said, holding out his hand.

Thune tried to refuse, but Peter insisted. He pressed a shiny goldpiece into Thune's hand.

Thune bowed deeply. A real goldpiece! Again he bowed. However, in his eyes was a hint of suspicion, suspicion which had appeared when the young gentleman had told him that he was going to the castle to discuss some business with the countess.

Thune wondered. What kind of business did this man have with the lady who had just brought such impossible hardship on her people? Was this man whom he had taken into his house trustworthy? Perhaps he and other merchants like him were to blame for the trouble the farmers were in. But Thune shook the thought from his mind. Probably his suspicions were unfounded.

His noble guest had told him that he had visited the

28

old mill last night. Thune had not noticed that Master Peter hadn't answered when he had asked him if he had seen the ghost.

Now he watched his guest urge his horse forward along the road that slowly climbed toward the castle, winding first through the woods. High above the wooded hill the snow-crusted battlements of the castle glittered in the sun.

Thune shook his head. No, he had no right to suspect this man who sat so upright in the saddle. Someone who met your eyes so openly and calmly didn't deserve such distrust. Thune squeezed the large, round goldpiece in his huge fist.

In the distance Master Peter turned in the saddle to wave one last goodbye. Thune took off his cap and flapped it energetically. Then he turned to go back into his cabin.

Hi! What was this?

How did that gruesome thing get over his door? It was a dead bird—a raven. Only a dead raven. But it frightened him more than he was willing to admit. Why did one dead bird frighten him so? Thune forced himself to examine the bird more closely. It wasn't a completely black raven. Its breast and back were gray, though its wings were black.

Who could have hung that grisly thing there? And why? Thune stepped onto a wooden pail and took the bird down. Too bad he hadn't spotted it while Master Peter was still here. A sudden thought flashed into his mind and he stood motionless on the pail. Had Master Peter . . . ?

Of course not! But then someone else must have been skulking around the house last night—a stranger. An unpleasant thought.

Shielding his eyes against the glare, Thune scoured the distance for Master Peter. Yes, there he was. But he was nothing more than a dark speck. Thune waved the dead raven over his head to attract the rider's attention, but it was no use.

With a shudder he tossed the bird toward the shed.

The road to the castle wound higher and higher up the hill. Oscar lifted his powerful legs high and dug his hooves deep into the crunchy snow. No one who saw the horse loping along would have suspected that it had enjoyed only a few hours of rest overnight. Nor did the rider look like someone who had been roaming the woods last night. He rode lightly in the saddle to the rhythm of the cantering horse.

As they neared the castle gate, Peter slowed his horse to a walk. Oscar's hooves thumped hollowly on the drawbridge that led across the moat to a huge, ironclad door. Peter reined in before the arched gate and looked up at the massive walls towering above him. An invader would have a hard time capturing this castle. First there was a broad moat, and then a solid stone wall rising high out of the water. Behind that stood the castle itself with its imposing walls and towers. Although the battlements glittered like gold in the sun, the castle exuded a somber threat. Peter could easily understand that the simple farmers of the countryside below looked up at this enormous bastion and its inhabitants with awe and fear.

Had some watchman in the tower seen the stranger approaching? Or had the guard at the gate heard the clatter of hooves on the bridge? In any case, a small hatch opened in the large door and a sullen face appeared in the barred opening. It had a nose like a turnip and a long drooping moustache. Tied around the rude face was a red cloth that was knotted at the top. The two points of the cloth stuck up like rabbit ears.

Peter had to force back a grin at the comical sight. The man seemed to be nursing a terrible toothache. Two black, beady eyes glared at Peter from beneath bristly eyebrows.

"Whatcha want?"

Now Peter had no difficulty hiding his grin. Instead, he was trying to control his temper. He pretended not to notice the man's boorish manners.

"I have come a long distance to speak with your mistress, Countess Ravenhurst."

"You don't say. What's your name?"

"I have a letter from my father, Squire Bettelburg."

A grunt was the only answer. Then the face vanished and the hatch banged shut. Footsteps retreated on the other side of the door. Peter shrugged to himself and thought, "People don't seem very polite around here. You ask to borrow someone's knife and he growls at you. In the middle of the night someone else tries to tack you to a beam with a similar knife. And then another boor leaves a gentleman standing outside the castle gate like a common peddler."

Footsteps approached the other side of the door, followed by the sound of bolts sliding back. Turnip-nose opened one of the doors and Peter could ride inside.

Stables and sheds, interspersed with haystacks and small shacks, lined the outer wall of the courtyard. The gatekeeper with the rabbit ears and turnip nose told Peter to follow him. Peter dismounted and a soldier took Oscar by the reins to lead him to one of the open stalls. Peter was surprised at the number of men in the courtyard. Most of them were carrying crossbows and lances. Several stood around a fire, heating the round metal hoop of a wagon wheel. In a sheltered corner, two others sat in the sun fixing harnesses.

They all looked like wild, rugged men. Thune had told him of rumors that the countess had hired a lot of new soldiers. Well, the old woman had picked a motley-looking crew. What a scruffy band of scoundrels!

Peter followed his guide to a second drawbridge that spanned an inner moat. Now they entered the castle. A tall, narrow door led into a maze of dim passages and dark stairways. Peter was curious about the coming meeting. What sort of woman was the countess? How would she receive him?

At last the gatekeeper stopped at a tall, heavy door and knocked respectfully. A gentle, friendly voice answered from behind the door. Turnip-nose opened the door and stepped back to allow Peter to pass.

Peter entered the castle hall and heard the gatekeeper close the door behind him. Not much light fell through the arched and narrow windows, but by the glow of a fire burning on the hearth he saw the countess sitting in a carved oak chair with a high back. Over the fireplace behind her hung richly decorated weapons and shields. One of the countess's hands rested on a silver cane, and with her other, she motioned her visitor to come closer.

"Come over here," she said. "My eyes are getting bad and I'd like to have a look at you."

Peter advanced until he stood before her, and he bowed respectfully. As he felt the old woman examining him from head to foot, he took care not to show his own curiosity, but he studied her in turn. She was dressed completely in black. Her black lace cap revealed some snow-white hair, but the rest of her face was covered by a veil that hung down to her shoulders. Yet a calm restfulness radiated from the old woman. With a polite but friendly gesture of her cane, she pointed Peter to a nearby chair.

"What is your name, young man, and what is the purpose of your visit?"

Peter sat down. He told her who he was, and from beneath his fur coat he took the letter his father had sent with him. With a small bow he handed it to her. The countess broke the seal and read the letter attentively. When she was finished, she turned to her visitor.

"I assume you're familiar with the contents of this letter and that you've discussed the purpose of your journey with your father? As I understand it, your father wishes to buy the entire supply of hides and furs that I collect from the farmers in payment for their rent."

Peter nodded. "Yes, my father has empowered me, if you are agreeable, to bargain with you."

The countess thought a moment. "All right, I'm agreeable. And I hope we can reach a fair price."

In the discussion that followed, Peter's respect for the old woman grew greater and greater. With her clear insight, she was very capable of looking after the interests of her extensive possessions.

How many furs would be collected in payment for rent? She couldn't say yet. "No," thought Peter, "I can understand that. But going by the somber faces of the farmers in the inn, I'd guess she will make a sizeable haul. Why did she put the rents so high this year? Is she in trouble herself? What kind of trouble can it be?" Suddenly Peter felt guilty about benefiting from the farmers' hardship.

The countess told him that in a few days her men would pick up rent payments from the farmers, and she invited Peter to stay in the castle as her guest until then. Then she rapped her cane on the floor three times. Peter understood that this signalled the end of the visit. At almost the same moment a man appeared from behind some heavy drapes that hung in one corner of the room. As he made an exaggerated bow to Peter, Peter surmised that he was a servant, although his flashy clothes and extravagant manners were out of character. He made a poor impression on Peter. His face was too oily, his beard too pointed, and his nose too sharp. His dark eyes sized Peter up in one withering glance.

The countess said to the servant, "Will you take this gentleman out and show him a comfortable room. And see to it that all his needs are tended to."

HE servant with the pointed beard led Peter out of the castle hall and down a long passage to a spacious room. In the fireplace burned a skimpy fire; glancing toward it, the servant said, "I'll send someone to stoke up the fire for you and see to your needs."

"Thank you," said Peter. But he thought, "Do whatever you like, Dandy Dan, but if you think I'm just going to sit here by the fire like an old granny for the next few days, guess again. Today I'm going to pay another visit to that old mill—this time by daylight. When someone is so ornery as to throw a knife at me, I want to know why. I'm going to do a little investigating."

Peter dropped into a chair and stretched out his legs as though he didn't plan to move for at least an hour. Dandy Dan made a stiff bow and began to leave the room, but when he reached the door, Peter called out as if something had just popped into his mind, "That's right! I almost forgot: I have to go back to town. Rats! When I dined at the inn yesterday I left one of my saddlebags hanging on a chair."

Peter had gotten up as he explained and now he slipped past the servant, buckled up his fur coat and started down the passage. He didn't look back. After descending the dark stairs, he had some trouble finding the main corridor that led to the door where he had entered. But after a few false tries, he found himself outside. His horse was tethered under one of the lean-to shelters along the outer wall.

Swinging into the saddle, he rode toward the gate. Turnip-nose was still on guard. The man gave him a dismal look, his hand cupped over his swollen cheek. He opened the gate and Peter galloped out. Peter was eager to examine the old mill by daylight. There had to be an explanation for how the black apparition in the door-way had disappeared without leaving tracks in the snow.

Slowly Oscar descended the hill. Peter kept glancing back until he was sure that trees obstructed any watchman's view of him. When he was sure that he would be unobserved, he left the road and headed into the forest. He zig-zagged on, picking his way through the trees and undergrowth, hoping to stumble across some landmark to tell him where he was.

Suddenly he once again heard the distant sound of rushing water. He was headed in the right direction. At last he reached the clearing of the old mill. Sliding from the saddle, he tied Oscar to a branch and walked across the clearing.

The mill looked deserted. Cautiously he approached the door, which still stood ajar. In the light of day, the building looked weatherbeaten and ordinary. Peter almost believed that last night's adventure had been no more than a bad dream. But the weight of the raven knife under his coat was no dream.

After carefully peeking around the door, he quickly stepped into the mill. It was rather dark inside; little light entered through the small cobwebbed window in the side wall. However, the large broken millstone in the middle of the floor was clearly visible. Beside it lay a heavy triangular wooden block. A mouse frightened by Peter's presence fled behind the huge stone. Peter kept glancing back at the door. After last night's surprise meeting, he was determined not to be ambushed again.

Reaching the ladder that led upstairs, he cautiously began to climb. Carefully he eased his head through the opening and scanned the second story. It was deserted now, and looked as though it had been deserted for years.

Peter pushed himself up and walked around, exploring further, but all he found was a pile of old burlap sacks covered with years of dust. Long ago this floor must have been used to store sacks of grain, which were no doubt brought in through the large hatch in the front which reached down to the second-story floor. Actually it was no more than a rectangular hole because its doors had long ago fallen off or had been blown off by a storm. Now the sunlight streamed in through the large opening. Carefully Peter walked toward it and looked outside.

Suddenly his eyes narrowed to small slits and his breathing stopped. He was looking straight down at the door he had entered only a few minutes ago. Standing motionless in that doorway was a man. On his head was a broad-rimmed hat and from his shoulders hung a long black cloak. It was the black apparition from last night!

It was standing right where it had stood when it had hurled the knife at Peter's head. But this time it wasn't dark and this time Peter wasn't going to be caught by surprise. His attacker wasn't going to vanish mysteriously without leaving a trail this time! Peter clenched his fists and gritted his teeth. The blood pounded in his temples. Without taking time to think, he crouched and leaped . . .

He leaped down onto the black figure's shoulders. Not expecting this sudden violent attack, certainly not from above, the man crashed to the ground, falling flat on his back. Peter rolled and scrambled back to his feet. The black figure was also starting to rise, but before he could get his legs under him, Peter knocked him down again. The momentum of his own blow caused Peter to stumble and fall to his own knees. Sitting on his knees, Peter again cocked his fist, as hard as a hammer and with the muscles of his arm tight as a bow behind it. As his opponent began to rise again, Peter prepared to strike.

Suddenly the broad-rimmed hat of the black phantom tumbled into the snow. Peter's arm went limp at his side, and his jaw dropped in amazement. A mass of thick, blond hair cascaded down over the shoulders of the black cloak. The winter sun seemed to strike sparks of gold from the blond shower of hair. Two blue eyes looked at him in terror. Kneeling before him in the snow was . . . a girl!

And she was a pretty girl. Peter guessed she couldn't be much older than twenty.

"Oh—" said Peter.

"Oh—" said the girl.

Despite his confusion, Peter couldn't help laughing—partly in relief. But the girl didn't even smile. She sprang to her feet and brushed the snow off her cloak, keeping a close eye on Peter. Her eyes showed both fear and uncertainty.

Feeling that he had to say something, Peter asked, "Did you hurt yourself?"

When he heard himself say it, he realized how silly it sounded. He had dropped on her with all his weight and clobbered her. Of course he must have hurt her. But the girl didn't answer, and her eyes met his for only an instant. He saw that they were wet. Was she crying? No. Had she been crying earlier?

She took a couple of steps backwards, and then, before Peter realized it, she had whirled and was running back toward the woods, limping slightly as she ran. Waiting for her in the trees was a gray horse. The girl quickly pulled the reins free and swung into the saddle. Her black cloak fluttered behind her as she sped away.

For a moment Peter considered pursuing her. But he didn't. Stooping, he picked up the broad-rimmed hat lying in the snow at his feet. Turning it in his hands, he examined it. Could this girl have been the one who—?

No. He shook off the thought. That was ridiculous. The mysterious figure in the doorway last night had been tall and broad-shouldered. Besides, it had come and gone without leaving a single footprint in the snow. Now two sets of tracks ran between the mill and the place in the woods where the girl's horse had been tethered. But why had she come to this isolated mill? And why had she dressed herself in this black hat and that long black cloak so that she looked like a man?

A whinny from Oscar startled Peter out of his ponderings. His horse was becoming impatient. Oscar must have heard the girl's horse running off, and that had made him restless. Peter unfastened one of the buttons of his coat and tucked the hat inside it. Deep in thought, he returned to his horse and rode away.

Strange things were happening to him. Last night he had come away from the old mill carrying a knife with a black raven on the handle. Now, less than half a day later, he was riding away with a hat under his coat. A few minutes ago the hat had covered a mass of golden hair. He felt the hat brim under his elbow and pressed it to him so that it wouldn't slip away. He didn't want to lose this memento of such a strange adventure.

He rode through the forest, trusting his luck. After a while, however, he began to ask himself whether he was headed in the right direction. He wasn't sure. A squirrel fled to the top of a tall pine. At last, however, light breaking through the trees ahead told Peter that he was nearing the edge of the forest.

Emerging from the trees, he looked around. Too bad: he had been off course. Thune's house was nowhere to be seen. Taking a guess, Peter began skirting the edge of the forest to look for it.

After riding a while, he spotted a low, sloping roof through the trees. It wasn't Thune's cabin, however. As he neared it, he saw an old man sawing wood near the shed. The man had also spotted him. He started in curiosity and politely lifted his cap to his visitor. His long beard was almost as white as the snow.

Peter reined in his horse and greeted the man, "Good morning. I'm afraid I'm lost. Tell me, how do I get to Thune's house from here?"

The old man put down his saw and painfully

straightened his back. "You're quite close to Thune's house. Look, if you cross that field to the end of that outcropping of trees, you'll see his house ahead of you."

A hint of a smile appeared on the old man's face, carved into deep furrows by the sun and the wind, as he asked, "Did you sleep well last night, sir?"

Peter raised his eyebrows in surprise. How did this man know—? But then he understood. Now he remembered where he had seen the old man before. He had been one of the farmers at the inn. He knew that Peter had spent the night at Thune's cabin.

"Yes, thank you," he replied. " I slept well, but not long."

Why had the old man asked him how he'd slept? Did he know about his nighttime excursion to the old mill? Was he—? No, of course not. His question was merely polite small talk.

"My night was short," Peter explained, "because Thune and I talked until far into the morning. He told me about the hardship brought on the local people and about the strange things that have been happening here."

Peter saw anxiety flicker in the old man's eyes.

"Yes, sir. So you know about the injustice that is being done us. Yes, that's what it is—a shameful injustice!"

He ran his hand over his white beard. "And do you know what the strangest thing is? I don't understand it. My father rented this farm from old Count Ravenhurst. He was the countess's father. When I was a boy, the countess was a little girl. She used to ride past often in a carriage drawn by four white horses.

"Once I was working out in the field with my father

when she came riding by. I'll never forget it. She saw me standing there, so I quickly took off my cap. Then she waved at me and smiled. I have loved and respected the countess ever since. And although it may sound strange, I still do."

The old man sat down on a chunk of wood and went on. "No matter who you talked to, castle servants or soldiers, they all spoke well of her. But now . . . ? Now this!" The old man shook his head. "No, I don't understand it."

Peter had listened attentively. Yes, it was strange. What was behind the countess's sudden harsh demands? He would have liked to ask the old man about the old mill, but he didn't know how to do so without arousing suspicion.

So he said goodbye and went on his way. He felt the old man's eyes on his back until he had passed out of sight behind the trees.

Following directions he soon came to Thune's cabin near the edge of the woods. He rode straight to it and led his horse into the lean-to. Suddenly Thune rushed around the corner of the house, flushed with excitement.

"Master Peter, am I ever glad you're back! After you left this morning I tried to call you back but you were too far away. Look what I've got."

Thune took a few steps, and then he stooped and picked something out of the snow. It was a dead bird—a gray raven. Its head and wings were black, but its body was gray. Dry blood was caked on its beak.

Peter looked at Thune quizzically. What was so unusual about a dead bird? Someone must have shot it.

And he had wanted to call him back for that?

"So?" he asked. "What about it? Where did it come from?"

Thune was obviously agitated. "I didn't see it before you left this morning, Master Peter. But when I turned to go back into the house, there it was, hanging over the door on a nail. I quickly took the awful thing down. Someone must have hung it there during the night. Brrr! I don't like all this grisly, spooky stuff!"

Peter rubbed his chin thoughtfully. Yes, it was strange—very strange.

Thune held the dead creature by one leg an arm's length away from himself. "No, this mysterious stuff doesn't agree with me. Do you think it was the gh-gh-gh—?"

The big man choked on the word, his frightened eyes flitting to the dark woods.

Peter smiled. "Do you think that the ghost of Ravenhurst Mill hung that dead raven over your door?"

Thune nodded and swallowed.

"Nonsense, Thune. You should know better. That ghost is just the product of fear and gossip."

"But, Master Peter, then who could have done it? And why?"

"Yes," thought Peter, "who did it and why?"

A sudden idea popped into his head. He stared off into the distance, trying to pull his thoughts together. Was it possible? Was there a connection between the dead raven and the raven on the handle of the knife that had been hurled at him? It seemed a little far-fetched. Besides, the raven on the knife was a black one and this one was gray. Still . . . many strange things had been happening around here. It wasn't impossible. Would he ever find out what was really going on?

ATE that afternoon Peter arrived back at the castle. When he crossed the draw-bridge, to his surprise the door was opened by a strange man. Turnip-nose and his red bandage had disappeared.

A servant hurried forward and led Oscar to one of the larger stables in the courtyard. Another asked Peter to follow him. He was led straight to the room where Dandy Dan had led him that morning. The servant said that it was the countess's wish that he make himself as comfortable as possible.

Peter looked around. A generous fire was burning in the fireplace, and on a bulky oak table stood a bowl of fruit and a silver pitcher. He picked it up and sniffed. It was full of wine. The last gray light of the winter day filtered in through two tall windows.

Peter collapsed into a chair and put his feet up on the hearth to warm them. The servant, meanwhile, retreated and closed the door behind him. Peter looked around. This was where he would have to wait until the farmers had paid their rent. Peter scowled. The way the farmers were being treated was really unfair. Again he felt partly

44

to blame for their misery, because the more furs and hides and grain the farmers turned over, the better for him. But what could he do about the injustice to them?

He stretched out his hand and took an apple from the nearby table. When he reached for his knife, he remembered that he had lost it. Grinning, he reached into his jacket and took out the other knife—the knife with the black raven on the handle. After eating the apple, he stood up and stepped to the window. It was snowing again. Big flakes tumbled past the window and fell on the roofs below or sank into the black water of the moat. In the distance, snow swirled into the woods.

Peter was thinking. That ancient forest of black tree trunks concealed a mystery. What kind of mystery was it? Were the unfriendly wagon driver from whom he had borrowed a knife and the black phantom in the doorway of the old mill one and the same person?

Was the knife he had borrowed to fix his saddle and the knife that the phantom had hurled at him one and the same knife?

What about that moaning in the forest at night, those heart-rending wails? Were those human souls? It hardly seemed possible. Yet . . . what else could they be?

Peter didn't know. Why hadn't the black figure left any footprints in the snow? It had vanished like a ghost. But he didn't believe in ghosts. Yet—?

Peter shook his head. He walked back to the fireplace and tossed two more pieces of wood onto the fire. Settling back in his chair once more, he sat and stared into the flickering flames for a long time, deep in thought. The darkness of the coming night stole out of the corners of the room and gathered around him.

He thought of the girl he had met that morning so unexpectedly. He smiled. A ridiculous scene, really—

that jump. Only now in the pleasant warmth of the fireplace did he feel how tired he was. He didn't even know her name . . .

Peter's head nodded forward. She certainly had a beautiful head of hair . . . Peter's eyelids fell shut. On his lips lay a faint smile.

A man lumbered through the dark corridors of the castle. He had small, beady eyes, a long, droopy moustache, and a red cloth binding his jaw and head. On the fingertips of Turnip-nose's hand rested a sumptuous meal spread on a silver tray. The light from the candalabra that he carried in his other hand cast an enormous shadow of his shaggy head on the wall of the corridor. The shadow looked like a giant seal with horns —the ends of the red cloth that stuck up above his ears.

Stopping at one of the doors, he kicked at it with the toe of his boot. When he heard nothing from the other side of the door, he gave it one more vicious kick and then, pushing down the handle with his elbow, he shoved the door open and stepped inside.

Peter had been wakened by the last hard knock. Startled, he blinked into the candlelight. Had he fallen asleep? For how long? He straightened himself in his chair and then saw Turnip-nose standing in the doorway. The man came in and set the silver tray and the candalabra on the table.

Gruffly he said, "Here's supper."

Peter looked at him. The man acted as if he were bringing food to a prisoner. A glance at the tray, however, showed Peter that the food was fit for a prince. Strangely enough, Peter didn't feel at all irritated by the man's rude manners. He sensed that his

unpolished manners were part of the man's character and not meant to insult him.

Suddenly Turnip-nose's expression changed. He was staring at the table. When Peter followed his gaze, he saw that the man's eyes were fixed on the knife with the black raven on the handle. Why was Turnip-nose staring at it so wide-eyed?

Peter scolded himself. It had been stupid of him to leave the knife lying out after he had eaten the apple. By Turnip-nose's face he could tell that the man not only recognized the knife, but that it had some special significance to him. Strange! Very strange indeed! But even stranger were the words that Turnip-nose spoke next. His voice sounded respectful, even humble, as he asked, "Are the ravens still black, sir?"

The odd question took Peter by surprise. Momentarily he was confounded, but he recovered at once and replied, "Yes, the ravens are black."

His answer had been a stab in the dark. Had he guessed right? Had he given the right answer?

He glanced at Turnip-nose out of the corner of his eye. What did this man know? What was he thinking? Was this an unexpected chance to lift a corner of the veil that shrouded so many mysteries? What did this puzzling exchange mean?

Suddenly he understood. "Are the ravens still black?"—that had to be a password. Had his reply been the right one? Everything now hinged on his guess. Again he studied Turnip-nose's expression. It betrayed an uneasy tension.

"Aah . . . I'm sorry, sir . . . You see, I didn't know that you—I mean, I wasn't sure—I thought—"

Numerous thoughts flashed through Peter's mind. One thing was sure: this man had recognized the knife, most likely by the raven on the handle. It had to be a sort of sign. Peter had to know for sure. So he gambled. He picked up the knife by the point and held the handle under Turnip-nose's beady eyes.

"You weren't sure everything was on the up-and-up, and so you asked me for the password. Right?"

"Yes, sir. That's it, sir!"

Peter nodded. "Very good. One can never be too careful. I'll remember that."

Peter knew that he was playing a dangerous game. But it seemed to be working splendidly. Turnip-nose glowed with pleasure and tried to make up for his earlier rudeness. He moved the table closer and set the steaming plate before Peter. "Enjoy your supper, sir."

Peter puzzled over how to handle the man now. He had made important discoveries by sheer luck. Now he knew for sure that there was some connection between the mysterious happenings at the mill and the castle. And he also knew that some group was involved which used, "Are the ravens still black?" as a password.

Turnip-nose had to be a member of the group. "If I make friends with this man," thought Peter, "maybe I'll be able to find out more. I have to get behind this mystery, no matter what the risk." One thing was sure: sooner or later he'd settle the score with his ambusher. Without betraying his thoughts to Turnip-nose, he calmly began to eat.

Peter looked up from his plate. Turnip-nose was still standing beside the table. The man seemed to be dawdling on purpose. What did he want? Did he want to ask a question? Peter pretended he didn't notice his delay and went on eating. Sure enough, at last the man gathered enough nerve to speak.

"May I ask a question, sir?"

"Go ahead," answered Peter. "You can always ask."

"When are we going to leave this place? It's starting to bore me, this hanging around and waiting."

Peter nodded and gave him a chance to get the rest off of his chest.

"We haven't heard anything from the Black Leader for the last while either. The only time we see him is at night, and then he's here and gone."

Peter had to be careful not to say too much. He might trap himself. All he said was, "In a few days there'll be some changes and then there will be lots of action."

Turnip-nose grinned, and a few crooked brown teeth showed between the drooping ends of his moustache. He seemed relieved and started toward the door. Peter kept him a little longer by asking him to pour a cup of wine. When he put down the cup beside Peter's plate, Peter said, "Pour one for yourself too. We'll drink to the success of our enterprise."

Turnip-nose beamed. He lifted his cup high, saying, "May we make a big haul."

"Aha!" thought Peter. "So there's plunder involved."

"Cheers!" he said.

THUNE'S cabin was nearly dark. The last small flames in the fireplace cast a faint, rosy glow against the ceiling beams. The big man sat at the window waiting. From time to time he wiped the frost from the window with his shirt sleeve and peered across the moonlit fields of snow. The darkness between the trees of the forest seemed to scowl at him. He shuddered —with cold or fear?

He had no idea how long he'd been sitting there. Sometimes he glanced over his shoulder into the room. As the fire in the fireplace slowly died, dark shadows crept out from the corners of the room as if stalking him. Thune shivered.

Yonder in the dark woods the terrible thing would happen. He was almost afraid to think of it. At midnight; that's when it could come. Just as horrible, just as eerie, and yet just as unexpectedly as the other nights— the wailing from Ravenhurst Mill.

Thune was startled out of his fearful thoughts. Had he heard something? What could it have been? It sounded like a soft, crunching sound in the snow outside. Yes, there it was again. It was coming closer. What could it be? What would be coming toward his cabin at this time of the night? No one was out this late.

Thune was afraid to look, but he couldn't help himself. Past the house rode a wagon pulled by two horses. But it was the driver who caught his eye. His grotesque head was very large and lopsided and had two large horns. Sweat beaded on Thune's forehead.

Then the man turned slightly and Thune saw that he was no freak. But on his shoulder sat a large black bird —a raven. Where had the man come from and where was he going at this time of night? Had he hauled something away, or was he coming to pick something up?

The wagon was empty. Thune didn't know the man; he had never seen him before. He was certainly no one from this area. Besides, what would a farmer be doing out near midnight? The wagon had come from the swamp. Slowly it rolled on by, the wheels crunching softly in the snow.

Thune's teeth chattered. This morning he had been badly frightened by that dead raven hanging over his door, and now a live raven went riding by on the shoulder of a mysterious stranger. The wagon moved on until it disappeared behind the trees. Was the driver following the edge of the woods to the castle?

Thune waited. The wagon with the mysterious driver had long since disappeared, but Thune was still waiting. Brrr! Seeing that raven had given him the willies. Good thing he had put an extra chain on the door and nailed the window shut.

That morning when Master Peter had returned from the castle and Thune had shown him the dead raven, the young man had looked very grave for some moments. A deep furrow had appeared in his forehead and suddenly he had said, "Thune, you're a sturdy fellow. I need your help. I want to find out what kind of ghost it is that haunts the old mill. Since it begins wailing about midnight every night, it should do so tonight too. I have to go back to the castle now, because I'm to stay there for several days. I can't hear the wailing from there, but I can see your house. Next time the ghost begins to wail, hold a lighted candle in your window and move it from side to side."

Thune had promised to help. Now he sat at the window waiting. The candle was lit so that it would be ready when he needed it. It was standing on the floor in a corner of the room so that it wouldn't shine through the window. As Thune grew sleepy, all sorts of weird images flitted through his mind. His head began to grow heavy and nod. It slowly sank forward and his eyes fell shut.

But vaguely he still saw something. What was that black thing sitting on the back of that stool? Was it a raven? And, look, on the corner of the table, another raven! And another on the mantel over the fireplace. Where did all those horrid ravens come from? How awful! The whole room suddenly seemed to be filled with black flapping wings, wicked eyes like glistening coals, and gaping, reaching bills. "Caw! Caw! Ca-a-aw!"

Thune tried to cry for help. He opened his mouth wide, but not a sound came out. But then suddenly a cry did reach his ears.

With a shock Thune woke up. Had he been dreaming? Yes, he must have been. Confused, he looked about. The ravens had vanished. But the screeching went on; it was no dream. The stillness of night in the forest was broken by those pitiful wails.

Meanwhile, at the castle, it was also late at night. Turnip-nose stood in the cold, vacant corridor, leaning against a doorpost. His eyes were a bit crossed as they focused on the end of his red nose. He was thinking. He didn't fully understand his orders. His orders were: "See to the guest's every need, but don't let him out of your sight."

Turnip-nose mulled it over. Why was it necessary to watch the young Bettelburg? After all, he was one of them, wasn't he? The knife with the raven on the handle was proof to that, and he had known the password. No, Turnip-nose didn't understand it.

Peter sat in his room near the fire, waiting for midnight. Sometimes he stood up to look out the window. He stared over the dark woods and the surrounding fields. Now and then when the moon peeked through the clouds, the night seemed etched in silver. After looking for a while, he went back to his chair by the fire, because it was still too early for the signal he was looking for.

Time dragged by. All at once he lifted his head to listen. A vague noise had reached his ears. Quietly he arose. Had the noise come from the courtyard, or from the corridor outside his door? Carefully he stepped to the window and looked outside. At first he saw nothing, but just as he was beginning to think that he had been mistaken and that the sound had come from the corridor after all, a black shape emerged from the shadow of the gateway. Again Peter heard the faint sound—the sound of wheels crunching in the snow. A wagon arriving at the castle this time of night?

His curiosity aroused, he watched carefully. Then,

with a sudden jerk, he turned toward the door. This time he definitely had heard something in the corridor. Was someone standing on the other side of his door? He frowned. Careful not to make a sound, he crept forward. With a quick jerk, he swung open the door.

Peter found himself staring into the startled face of Turnip-nose. Peter was also surprised, but he tried not to show it. The pot-bellied servant almost lost his balance. He caught himself just in time to keep from tumbling into the room. He opened his mouth to speak but seemed at a loss for words.

Peter, however, was in full command of himself. He acted as though it was not at all peculiar to find Turnip-nose lurking on the other side of the door. Calmly he asked him to fetch some more firewood because the fire was burning down.

Turnip-nose was visibly relieved that he wasn't asked to explain his presence in the corridor. Hurriedly he disappeared down the hall. Standing at the open door, Peter thought quickly. He was rid of the pesky servant for awhile, which was excellent, for Thune's signal might come at any time, and then he had to be free to act. Tonight at the old mill he would settle the score with the black apparition. He snatched the knife from the table and stepped into the corridor. Quietly he closed the door behind him.

Ahead and around the corner were the stairs that led to the main entrance, but his route was shrouded in darkness. A torch at the opposite end of the corridor was the only light. A host of thoughts milled through his mind. Could he get away before Turnip-nose returned? Could he make it to his horse without being seen?

Would he be able to get through the gate? Turnip-nose would find the room empty when he returned with his load of wood, but never mind. He'd invent some story that the man would swallow.

Peter stopped at the top of the stairs. They ran into the corridor below, which led to the main entry door. On each side of the entry burned a torch. Peter set his foot on the top stair, but then he quickly pulled it back.

The latch on the main door rattled, the door opened, and someone stepped inside. Peter held his breath and retreated as far as possible into the shadows of a shallow niche, keeping his eyes on the door. Downstairs a man moved into the full light of the two torches and looked around. He wore the rude clothing of a local farmer and his face looked hard and grim. Peter started. He had seen this man before! He was the wagon driver he had met in the woods—the man who had lent him the knife to repair his cinch, the knife with the raven in the handle. What was he doing here at the castle?

Over his arm hung a gray blanket and on his shoulder sat a raven. The bird spread its wings wide and opened its beak: "Caw!" And eerily, hollowly an answer echoed out of the vaulted darkness: "Caw!" Peter could tell that the bird's wings had not been clipped. Since it did not fly off, it had to be well-trained.

Peter didn't have much time to stand around wondering what the man was doing here, for the wagon driver quickly strode up the corridor toward the stairs. Swiftly Peter took a few steps backward, looking around in the dark hallway. Where could he hide? Could he make it back to his room? Heavy footsteps sounded on the stairs. No, he could no longer reach his room unseen.

The man's head would appear at the top of the stairs at any moment.

As he swiftly retreated, Peter's hands groped along the wall. Was this a doorpost? No time to hesitate. His hand found a doorknob.

Fortunately the door wasn't locked. Quickly he opened it just far enough to slip inside and closed it quietly behind him. Just in the nick of time. Already the footsteps were at the top of the stairs. But what if the man came to this very room? Peter stepped behind the door and listened, hardly daring to breathe. The footsteps approached and passed by without pausing. Their sound died away at the end of the hall.

Only then did Peter look around. The room was dark. Through a tall, arched window fell a long column of moonlight. Peter pressed his ear against the door to listen. Was it safe to venture out into the corridor?

Suddenly his heart lurched with a new fright. In the dark room behind him, something scraped—as if a chair had been moved. He spun around. Just then a bright flash dazzled his eyes. Someone lit a candle with a tinder-box.

Peter's eyes widened in astonishment.

HERE, at the other end of the room stood a girl—the girl he'd met that morning, the girl from the old mill. Peter could hardly believe his eyes. For the second time within moments, he had met someone whom he hadn't at all expected to meet in the castle. The girl stood motionless behind the table. Her blue eyes, riveted on him with fright and amazement, were hooded by a dark shadow.

Recovering from his astonishment, Peter took a step forward and said, "Excuse me for stepping into your room without knocking. I didn't know anyone was in it." His words sounded strange to his own ears. But he could hardly tell her he was hiding from a wagon driver with a raven. That would require too much explanation.

He took two more steps toward the table, feeling that he nevertheless owed her some kind of explanation. She still looked alarmed and suspicious. He could understand her fear, but it made him feel badly. His first encounter with her couldn't have made her feel kindly toward him. Yet he sensed that they were not necessarily enemies in this confused adventure into which she, too, seemed to have been drawn against her will.

58

What kind of thoughts about him were going through her head? Peter wanted to reassure her. Should he tell her everything honestly and openly? Perhaps that would allay her suspicions. He knew that to do so would be taking a great risk, but he wanted to try.

Smiling, he took a few more paces toward her. She still stared at him without moving. "I haven't had a chance to introduce myself," he began. "I am Peter of Bettelburg. I'm afraid I gave you quite a scare this morning."

Now she made a slight movement with her head, and in the yellow candlelight her hair shimmered like gold. Peter told her why he was staying at the castle and what the purpose of his visit was. He also told her about the nightly moaning and wailing in the woods and about Thune's fear. More and more spilled out as he talked on and on: about his first visit to the old mill and the black apparition he had glimpsed in the moonlit doorway for a split second; about the knife that had buried itself in a beam a few centimeters from his ear; about this morning when he had gone to the mill to investigate and how he had taken her for the black apparition. "And that is why I jumped you," he finished.

The girl had listened motionlessly, but gradually fear and suspicion had left her eyes. Peter went on. He told her about the unfriendly driver who had lent him a knife with a black raven on the handle and that he had just spotted the same man in the corridor. "That's why I stepped into your room: I didn't want him to see me."

Peter paused and thought a moment. Then he plunged on. "Perhaps you could help me."

The girl's eyebrows shot up. "Me . . . ?"

"Yes," said Peter. "I've told you my story. Now you tell me yours."

The girl hesitated for a moment. Then she asked, "What's there to tell?"

Peter said nothing. He just waited. At last she began to talk. "I have also noticed strange things happening around the castle lately. But I really don't know how I could help you."

She motioned him to a low bench. Swinging his sword behind him, Peter sat down. "You could begin by telling me who you are and why you went to the old mill this morning," he said.

Again she wavered, but then she overcame her doubt. "My story isn't nearly as exciting as yours. Except that I had someone drop down on top of me out of the sky."

For the first time Peter saw a glimmer of a smile on her lips.

"But I guess I should begin at the beginning. My name is Alma and this castle is my home. The countess is my grandmother." She frowned as if her thoughts pained her.

"Grandma and I get along very well. She has always been very kind to me and I love her very much. But . . . but . . ." she paused, searching for the right words. When she went on she seemed almost to be talking to herself. "Oh, it's all sad and confused. I don't know what it is, but it must be something that causes Grandma much grief. I used to see a lot of her. We always dined together in the main hall. She's the only family I have. My mother died and my father was killed a long time ago in battle."

She stared off into space for some moments and brought a lace handkerchief to her eyes.

"Now Grandma keeps to her room for several days in

a row, refusing to see anyone. Not even me. I wish I knew what was bothering her. And there's something else too. She has dismissed all the regular castle guard and replaced them with strange, rude soldiers. They guard the castle as if Grandma were expecting an attack.

"Despite her poor back, twice she has climbed the long stairs to the main tower to look out over the fields. She must have hired those strange soldiers because she expects trouble. It must cost her a lot of money, and once she told me that because of poor harvests the income from the farms hasn't been enough even to meet expenses.

"And . . . and all I can do is sit in my room and worry without being able to do a thing. Oh, I wish I could help Grandma!"

She stopped.

Wanting her to go on, Peter prompted, "But you went to the old mill this morning."

"Yes," she said, "that's true. One of the kitchen girls told me about the ghost."

"Why did you go to the mill? Certainly not because of ghost stories told by simple, superstitious people?"

"No," answered the girl. "You're right. I had another reason. All the strange events of the last week made it hard for me to go to sleep last night, so I got up and sat at the window without lighting a candle. It must have been about midnight when someone rode out of the shadow of the castle toward the main gate. Someone must have been on guard there, because the doors opened and the man rode toward the woods and vanished into the darkness."

Peter listened very attentively now.

"After some time the rider returned. I couldn't see his face from up here, but I'm sure it was the same man. I recognized him by his long black cloak and broad-rimmed hat. He frightened me, and I wanted to go to Grandma's room to tell her what I had seen. But when I got to where the corridor turns, I heard quiet footsteps ahead. It sounded like someone in heavy boots trying to steal down the hall without making any noise. I raced back to my room and crawled into bed."

She swept back her hair.

"This morning, in the light of day, I recovered my courage. I began to think that there might be some connection between the ghost stories told by the farmers and the mysterious rider who left the castle at midnight. I decided to go to the mill to see whether I could find any clues. The kitchen girl got me a long cloak and a hat so I could do it without being recognized. She also helped me leave the castle without being seen. There's a small gate in the rear of the castle with a little drawbridge. It's hardly ever used, but it still works."

Now she smiled quite freely.

"Well, you know what happened on my little excursion."

The room fell silent. Peter sat and thought, his hand under his chin. At last he broke the stillness. "Your story has been a great help to me. I think we can safely assume that the rider you saw leaving the castle and the black apparition that hurled his knife at me are one and the same person. That means we must look for the key to this mystery here in the castle."

Peter rose to leave. Then he remembered something. Unbuttoning his coat, he reached into his tunic and pulled out the flattened hat. Holding it out to the girl, he said, "This is yours. But if I were you, I wouldn't use it

again. It's too dangerous for you to go snooping about
by yourself . . . And one other thing. If you see anything
that looks strange or suspicious, let me know as soon as
you can. Even if you don't think it's important.
Agreed?''

"Agreed.''

They shook hands. Then Peter stepped to the door.
"Better put out the candle,'' he said. Carefully opening
the door a crack, he listened for noises in the corridor. It
seemed to be safe. He slipped out of the room and quietly shut the door behind him.

The torch at the end of the hall had been extin-
guished; he found himself standing in total darkness.
What should he do now?

His visit with Alma had taken a lot of time. No doubt
the wailing at the mill had already happened by now and
Thune had already signalled from his window. What
would he say if he knew his vigil had been in vain?

Peter didn't hesitate long. He made up his mind. Instead of returning to his room, he cautiously stole down
the stairs to the big door. He was in luck: it wasn't
locked. Quietly he stepped outside. Moonlight and large
blocks of shadow alternated along the walls of the courtyard. Peter pressed himself into a dark corner, for at
the gateway he had seen the silhouette of a man. Was it
the gatekeeper? Too bad! Now he hadn't a ghost of a
chance to leave the castle unseen. Suddenly, however, he
remembered Alma's mention of a rear gate out of the
castle.

After waiting until the man at the gate turned his
back, he ran toward the far side of the castle. Then he
crept along the sloping bank of the moat, using it as

cover. What if someone spotted him from one of the castle windows? What explanation would he give if they caught him, the honored guest of the countess, sneaking about in the dark like a thief? Peter put it out of his mind. It was a chance he had to take.

The stone wall rose massively from the black water of the moat. Here and there a silver film of ice glistened on the water. The black pinnacles of the castle towers pointed high into the starry night sky. Peter followed the moat until he reached the rear of the castle, where he began searching for the small gate Alma had mentioned. He soon found it.

This side of the castle, opposite the moon, was completely in shadow. Peter had to grope all over the door to find the bolts. Then, very slowly, so that the old hinges didn't creak, he pushed the door open.

Suddenly he leaped aside, his heart racing in fright. Something had brushed past his leg and had darted through the partially opened gate. Peter threw out his hands to keep from falling against the wall. Across the small drawbridge shot a low black shape. What was it? A dog? What else could it be?

When it broke clear of the shadow cast by the castle, he saw it silhouetted against the snow. Sure enough, it was a large black dog. Why was it running away from the castle? It vanished into the darkness of the forest. Peter shrugged; he didn't understand it, but he had other things to worry about.

After setting the door ajar so that it wouldn't latch, he crossed the drawbridge and followed the outer moat until he reached the front of the castle. Near the large drawbridge of the main gate, he stopped. Chewing his lip thoughtfully, he studied the snow. The hoofprints in the snow gave a clear message. Since it had snowed earlier that evening, these had to be recent. There were two sets of tracks. One led away from the castle gate. The other set returned; the rider had come back from the woods to the gate. Were these the tracks of the mysterious rider that Alma had seen?

Again Peter chewed his lip. If they were, it would be senseless for him to continue with his plan; the man had already returned to the castle.

Careful to avoid detection, he returned the way he had come. Soon he was back in his room. Turnip-nose was nowhere to be seen. Peter breathed a sigh of relief. Quickly he undressed and crawled into bed. It had been a long evening.

THE next morning a heavy-set man slogged through the deep snow in the woods. The collar of Thune's coat was pulled high around his face; only his eyes were visible under his knit cap. They looked grim and worried. He glanced up. Between the bare branches fell the first large flakes of another snow squall. Would he make it before the snow came? He had to! After all, he had promised Master Peter. Hastily he plowed on, for a promise was a promise. No one could say that Thune didn't keep his word.

Early that morning Master Peter had come to his house. In the half-light, he, Thune, had not even been dressed yet. He'd been still standing at the fireplace in his red longjohns stirring his oatmeal when suddenly someone had banged on the door.

Thune had dropped the spoon into the pan in fright, thinking that perhaps there were hoodlums at his door. But when he saw Master Peter's tall black horse outside the window, he quickly slid back the bolts of his door to let Peter in.

"Good morning, Master Peter. Did you see my signal

last night? When that awful sound started in the woods, I waved the candle at least four times.''

Without replying, Master Peter put a letter on the table. It was a very official looking letter with a red seal on it. "Thune," asked Master Peter, "will you do me a big favor? This letter must go to a ship in the harbor of the city on the coast. Would you bring it to the tollhouse on the hessian road for me? The mail coach will take it from there.''

Thune had picked up the letter by one corner very carefully for it lay right beside a piece of sausage. After tucking it safely inside his shirt, he had hunted up his pants and boots.

Now Thune had been traveling for some time. Again he checked the sky. If the snow held back just a little longer, maybe he could reach the tollhouse before the mail coach arrived. If it didn't snow too much, perhaps he could make it back home late tonight. At least he wouldn't have to pass the old mill. The thought sent a cold shiver down his spine. Resolutely he plodded on.

Suddenly he stopped. Turning his head, he listened closely, trying to peer through the gray swirl of snow. What was that sound he had heard? Was it a wolf?

No, a wolf-howl was more piercing. Thune's hand seized the handle of the long hunting knife strapped to his belt. He wasn't afraid—not if it was something he could see. What scared him were those eerie, unworldly happenings of late, things he couldn't see or understand.

On his guard now, he walked on. The sound had come from directly in front of him. When he rounded a bend in the forest path, he spotted a dark shape in the swirling snow ahead. It was an animal about the size of a wolf. But it wasn't a wolf; as Thune approached, it looked up and wagged its tail.

A dog! What was a dog doing out here in the woods far away from people? The dog was carrying something in his teeth. As Thune drew closer, he started with shock. Was it a—did he see right?—was it a human leg?

Very cautiously he edged a little closer. No, of course it wasn't a leg; it was only an empty boot. Thune put away his knife and patted the big dog on the head. The shaggy tail wagged joyfully.

Why was this dog out here in the woods? To Thune's knowledge there were no homes or farms anywhere in the area. The dog began digging in the snow. Was he looking for something? Had he lost his master? Had the dog found one of his master's boots? Thune shook his head. That seemed awfully unlikely. How could anyone lose such a tall boot? Impossible!

Thune kicked some of the snow aside to see if he could uncover something, but he wasn't very hopeful. If the dog with his keen nose couldn't find it, certainly he didn't stand much of a chance.

The dog had dropped the boot in the snow and nuzzled the bulging pocket of Thune's coat. Thune smiled. He knew what the dog was after. He smelled the bread and bacon in his pocket. Thune took out some bread and broke off a big piece.

"Here you go, you beggar."

The dog devoured it in a single bite.

Thune looked around. The snow seemed to be letting up a little. He couldn't waste any more time here; he had to hurry on. But he couldn't leave the dog alone in the middle of nowhere. It would perish from cold and hunger.

"Come on, boy, follow me!" he said, moving on.

The dog hesitated a moment. Then it picked up the boot and trotted after Thune.

Thune looked back and smiled. "Attaboy! You just stick with me. We can both use the company."

Afternoon was ending and the early dusk of winter was creeping in. In his small cabin, his chair close to the fire, an old man sat deep in thought. Leaping flames threw a rosy glow over his white beard. A long life of hard work had carved deep grooves in his weathered face. He was stirring an iron pot that hung over the fire. Anxiety lurked in his eyes. Sometimes he shook his head. What had happened? What had made the countess so cruel all of a sudden? Why was she taking almost everything from her poor, hard-working people?

He asked himself whether his granddaughter would visit him today. Probably not, for it would soon be dark. From time to time he glanced out through the window, scanning the edge of the woods. No one in sight. His granddaughter was a kitchen maid in the castle, and sometimes she was sent to the village to run errands. Then she always stopped at her grandfather's house.

Someone hammered on the door. The old man started. Who was that pounding so violently? That couldn't be his granddaughter.

"Open the door! Come on, we haven't got all day!"

The old man lurched to his feet. Looking out the window, he saw a wagon drawn by two horses standing in front of the house. What did this mean? Who could these men be? With trembling fingers he slid back the bolt on his door. Before him stood two strange men and on the wagon sat a third. What did they want from him?

"Hurry up, old man. Open the shed," ordered one of them. "We're from the castle. We've come to collect your rent. Come on, don't just stand there!"

The old man's heart sank with dread. What was the meaning of this? In other years the farmers had always delivered the rent to the castle themselves, and they usually did so at the end of the winter. But now three rough strangers came to his door shouting orders. Anger flamed up inside the old man's breast. His white beard trembled. "What do you—"

One of the men seized him by the shirt. "For the last time, open the shed and be quick about it!"

The other man prodded him in the back with a pike. Giving up, the old man trudged ahead of them to the shed. What choice did he have? He had no chance against three soldiers.

His clogs sank deep into the snow, but he felt no cold. As soon as he had unlocked the door of the shed, the two men rudely shoved him aside and went in. Stacked neatly in the gloomy interior were sacks of grain and precious furs—the fruit of a whole year's labor.

The men laughed and elbowed each other. Then they began to load the wagon. The old man stood at the door, looking on helplessly. His face had turned stiff and pale.

The men continued hauling for some time; and they didn't stop until the shed was empty. They didn't leave a single sack of grain or a single fur. Then the men leaped up onto the wagon, the driver shook the reins, and the horses threw their weight into the harness. The three men didn't even look back at the old man standing by his empty shed.

When the wagon had disappeared down the road, the old man slowly, numbly closed the door to his shed.

Further down the road was Thune's place. Would they empty his shed too? The old man shook his head. Defeated, he returned to his cabin.

"Grandpa!"

Running toward him from the woods came a teenage girl. The old man's face brightened. They both reached the door at the same time, and the girl kicked off her clogs. There was anger and sympathy in her eyes and her face was flushed.

"Grandpa, I saw everything. I was coming to see you, and when I saw those men, I hid behind a tree until they left. Grandpa, did they take—"

The old man had sat down on his chair near the fire. He interrupted her angry gush of words with a gentle wave of his hand. "Hush, child."

"But Grandpa . . . !"

"Come here and sit with me on this stool. Calm down. I want to get over my anger and you can help me do that."

"Yes, but Grandpa . . . !"

"Hush. You can help me by sitting there quietly and not saying a word. That's it."

With a weary gesture the old man stroked his beard. Each sat in silence with his own thoughts. It was the grandfather who finally broke the silence. "What just happened wasn't fair, was it?"

The girl shook her head.

"One thing you must always remember. Dishonesty and evil cannot last. Sooner or later whatever is built on injustice will crumble, for justice will overcome it. God is just."

The girl sat motionless and looked at the old man.

The anger she had seen in his eyes was now gone. She saw only peace and deep trust.

N THE light of the bright morning sun pouring in through the tall windows, Peter was enjoying the hearty breakfast that Turnip-nose had served him. Painting golden squares on the brown wood of the floor, the sun filled the room with a happy glow. Peter looked around. He knew that the happy glow was mere appearance. The sun couldn't remove the gloom of the castle. Hidden somewhere in the castle was a dark secret. But what could it be?

Turnip-nose seemed reluctant to leave the room. He rubbed his swollen cheek through the red kerchief and looked on enviously as Peter cut himself two thick slices of ham. Peter had noticed that the man was hanging on, and he suspected that he wanted to talk. But rather than encourage him, Peter ate in silence.

"Sir," began Turnip-nose, "I was here earlier this morning, but you weren't here."

"That's right," said Peter. "I went out for a ride early this morning. Last night I went out to check my horse because I noticed that he was limping a little yesterday. So I took him out this morning to put him through some paces. I think he needs a rest."

Peter thought, "There, that gives me two alibis at the same time. One for today and one for last night." And he could tell that Turnip-nose was now satisfied on both counts. The story about his horse limping wasn't a complete lie, because Oscar was indeed favoring one leg. However, the incident had actually happened this morning when Peter was on his way to Thune's house. Oscar had stumbled over a root hidden under the snow and had lost one of his shoes.

Turnip-nose rubbed his sore cheek again. His next remark showed that he believed Peter's story and was now going on to other matters. "I was supposed to ask you in the name of the countess if you would see her later this morning."

Peter nodded. "Of course."

With Peter silent again, Turnip-nose had no further excuse for staying. He said goodbye and left the room. A little later Peter buckled on his sword and went out for his audience with the countess. He was eager to find out what she wished to discuss with him.

As he walked down the corridor, he kept his eyes open for a glimpse of Alma. "Alma." He said the name softly to himself. A pretty name. But he reached his goal without seeing her.

The guard standing at the door of the main hall was just saying no, the countess was not in, when a strange thumping sound approached from around the corner of the corridor. Eventually the countess came around the corner, dressed in her black dress and veil and walking with her ebony cane. It was the cane that had been making the thumping sound on the floor. Thunk . . . thunk . . . . thunk! Slowly she walked up to him.

Peter bowed, and the guard opened the big doors. The countess greeted Peter, "Glad to see you here already, Master Peter." Leaning heavily on her cane, she shuffled into the castle hall. "Please follow me and make yourself comfortable." With a sigh she lowered herself into the tall chair with the carved back. Then she pointed Peter to a chair.

After asking Peter whether he was happy with his room and whether he had slept well, she got down to business. "Since the time has come for the collection of rents and since I do not wish to impose on your time any longer than is absolutely necessary, I feel we should finalize our agreement as quickly as possible."

Peter nodded. After a short discussion about prices, they came to an agreement satisfactory to both of them. Since the precise quantities to be collected from the farmers were not certain, Peter would make payment when everything was in his possession.

The countess looked bowed and weary. Alma was right; the old woman seemed to be weighed down by a great burden, but she was also trying hard to present a cheerful front to her guest and hide the worries harrying her. Peter's respect and sympathy for this frail but courageous woman almost prompted him to ask her openly what was bothering her. But he did not want to be rude.

And then there was another reason that he was watching his words. He could have sworn that once he had seen the heavy drapes behind her chair move ever so slightly. Was someone concealed behind them? Was someone eavesdropping on their conversation? Peter kept a wary eye on the drapes without betraying his suspicion.

The countess went on talking. "Oh yes. I've been

meaning to ask you whether you've made arrangements to transport what you've bought to your province.''

Before Peter could answer, the countess continued. ''If not, I have a proposal for you. I have access to two solid ships with experienced skippers. They are to depart for your province anyway to buy wares that we need here. If it fits in with your plans, it would not be necessary to bring the collected rents here to the castle. They can be carried directly from the farms to the river where my ships are anchored. It would save a lot of time and work.''

Peter mulled this over. He had made arrangements for transporting the goods he'd bought. But these could be changed. His eyes were caught by the drapes just then. Had they moved again?

''Yes,'' he heard himself saying, ''that sounds like an excellent arrangement.''

''You're a bright young fellow,'' she replied.

Then she fell silent and Peter gathered by this that she considered their meeting over. He arose and, as she had at the end of the last discussion, the countess rapped three times with her cane. He expected the servant with the pointed beard to appear from behind the drapes to show him out.

But the drapes didn't stir. Instead he heard a door opening at the other end of the room. When he turned, the oily fellow, standing behind him, bowed low. He had entered the hall through an almost invisible door, really not much more than a rotating panel in the oak-panelled wall. Peter studied the man discreetly. It seemed unlikely that this same fellow could have been listening behind the drapes. He couldn't have traveled from one end of the hall to the other that quickly. Still . . . was someone else hiding behind the drapes? If so, who? Or was the strange atmosphere of this place making his imagination run away with him? Perhaps a slight breeze had stirred those drapes.

Once again Peter noticed that the servant's dress was very stylish and expensive. The man seemed to weigh Peter in one penetrating glance. Again, although he could hardly say why, Peter felt strong dislike.

With a little bow, Peter said goodbye to the countess and followed the slick servant into the corridor. The man accompanied Peter to his room without saying a word. After opening the door, he bowed deeply once again and disappeared down the corridor.

Peter entered his room. He shrugged with irritation. That man bothered him. When he had bowed, Peter could have sworn that he had flashed him a false, taunting grin.

That afternoon Peter saddled his horse and rode to the river at an easy walk. He was curious about the ships the countess had mentioned. Oscar was favoring his right leg a little because his shoe was missing, but it didn't seem to bother him as he walked through the deep snow. The way to the river was easy to find, but when Peter reached the swamp, he had to keep a sharp eye out for dangerous spots. Smaller pools were coated by a thin layer of ice hidden under the snow. After crossing a vast field broken here and there by hairy plumes of willows, Peter suddenly came upon a set of deep ruts in the snow. They must have been made by heavily loaded wagons. He decided that they would probably lead him to the place where the ships were anchored.

His guess proved right. Soon he spied the two ships anchored close together, a stone's throw from the riverbank. Large gray ice floes floated sluggishly past their black hulks. From a distance he watched several men hauling furs and grain from wagons to a large raft made of tree trunks. When the raft was loaded, they pushed it to the ships with long poles. On the front of the raft stood a soldier who pushed ice floes out of the way with the end of his pike.

While Peter waited and watched, an empty wagon rumbled off and a full wagon drove up. When the raft had been unloaded it returned to shore for another load. Peter rode toward the river. Dismounting, he tied Oscar's reins to a bush. He greeted the men, and they mumbled something without stopping their work. When the raft was loaded, Peter jumped aboard and rode along to one of the ships.

Aboard ship he checked the pelts and hides and counted the sacks of grain. The furs were of prime quality. He hadn't expected to get so many. And one of the men said that there were still three wagonloads to come. What would his father say when he returned with this valuable cargo? The countess hadn't demanded a steep price from him.

Peter's delight, however, was spoiled by nagging uneasiness. He kept remembering the farmers in the inn and the despair he had seen in their faces. It was too bad his good fortune had to be at the expense of the people who had tramped the forests for these furs and had sweat to harvest this grain. If it had been up to him, he would have been just as happy with a smaller cargo. Those extra furs meant so much to these poor farmers—the difference between eating and going hungry . . .

Peter returned to shore with the raft and untied Oscar. Deep in thought, he followed his own tracks back to the castle. By the time he reached the castle, dusk was settling in. In his room, he sat down by the fire, still turning things over in his mind.

He was startled out of his ponderings by a rap on the door. It was his supper, brought by a strange servant, not by Turnip-nose. When Peter asked where the man with the toothache was, he was told that he was sleeping because it was his turn to stand watch at the gate tonight. The man set the meal and the silver wine jug on the table and left.

Supper finished, Peter stretched out in the easy chair with his feet near the fire and let the events of the last few days run through his mind once again. There had to be some way to lift the veil that shrouded everything in mystery. He felt frustrated, as if the key was somewhere near his fingertips, but he kept groping in the dark.

His first encounter with the mystery had been his run-in with the wagon driver who had lent him the knife with the raven on the handle. Had he really seen a boot among the branches on the wagon? It had been nearly dark. He could have been mistaken. But . . .

Then there were the angry, desperate farmers in the inn. Thune with his story about the ghost of Ravenhurst Mill. The eerie sound that had drawn him out to investigate the mill. The black apparition that had thrown a knife at him—a knife with a raven on the handle—and that had vanished without leaving tracks in the snow.

The next morning, after his first visit with the countess, he had met Alma in their strange encounter at the mill. And then Thune had told him about the raven hung over his door. That night he had almost run into the wagon driver with a live raven on his shoulder. This had led to his second encounter with Alma, who had told him about the black figure she saw leaving the castle the night before to return some time later. She had also said the countess seemed to expect some kind of danger. What was it that troubled the old woman so? Why had she climbed up to the tower to look out over the winter landscape?

Then there was the password he had tricked out of Turnip-nose: "Are the ravens still black?" What was the secret behind all these ravens? Peter couldn't find a way through the maze of questions.

It was late. Only the flames in the fireplace gave light to the dark room. The darkness seemed almost alive. Peter stood up and stretched. He was stiff from sitting still so long and his legs ached. Tonight he would try once again to reach the old mill without being seen. Would he find the solution to the mystery there? Or should he be looking here in the castle? Well, he would look until he found it.

Had Thune already returned from his long hike to the tollhouse? Had he delivered the letter in time? Peter buckled on his sword and donned his fur coat. Carefully he opened the door and peered up and down the corridor. It was empty.

**P**ETER descended the stairs and crossed the main foyer without meeting anyone. Approaching the big door, he was seized by the dread that it would be locked. Quietly he lifted the latch and pushed. He pushed again. At last the door moved. Slipping outside, he soundlessly closed the door behind him. He was outside the castle. In the shadow of the doorway he stopped to survey the courtyard. Faint moonlight silhouetted a man slowly pacing back and forth before the gate.

Calmly Peter crossed the bridge spanning the inner moat and strolled toward the man. The strange servant who had brought his supper tonight had been right; the guard was Turnip-nose. With his cloak and pike he looked even more comical than usual.

When Turnip-nose recognized him, he awkwardly attempted to stand at attention. Peter began chatting with him. "Evening! I just came out to get a breath of fresh air before turning in. Oh, yeah, I should also check on my horse's leg while I'm out here."

Peter noticed that Turnip-nose kept sticking his tongue into his sore cheek. Obviously his toothache was causing him much pain. Gradually a plan began to take shape in Peter's mind. Would it work?

"How's your tooth? Not so good, eh? It's amazing how one of those little grinders can ruin your life, isn't it? Did that glass of wine help you yesterday?"

Turnip-nose nodded. "Yes, sir, it sure did." His beady little eyes gleamed at the memory.

"I have an idea," said Peter. "The fire in my fireplace is burning low. Why don't you go up there and stir up a good blaze. Meanwhile, you can rinse your sore tooth a little. There's a big jug of wine on the table."

Turnip-nose's face beamed for a moment, but then it fell in chagrin. "Yes, sir, you see . . . I'd love to . . . But I can't leave my post. I'm supposed to guard the gate."

Peter acted as though this hadn't even entered his mind. He rubbed his jaw and looked thoughtful. "Tell you what: you go ahead; I'll take your place for awhile."

Turnip-nose looked shocked. "But . . . but—"

"No buts. It makes no difference who's on guard. Just give me your cloak and hat and pike. In the dark no one will see that I'm taking your place."

Turnip-nose's face brightened again. "But, sir, you can't stand on guard here just like a common soldier. It isn't—"

Peter laughed. "I told you I came for a breath of fresh air, didn't I? What difference does it make where I stand? Don't worry about me."

Turnip-nose was only too eager to be persuaded. Licking his lips at the thought of the wine, he quickly shed his cloak and draped it over Peter's shoulders. Peter also took the broad-rimmed leather hat and the long pike.

"Take your time," said Peter, but Turnip-nose was

already on his way to the castle. "Remember," shouted after him, "take a big mouthful to rinse your tooth and then swallow it in one gulp. Better rinse it several times."

The shadow of the castle swallowed Turnip-nose. Peter grinned. His plan had worked perfectly: he was rid of one pair of prying eyes. It would probably be some time before the man returned.

Peter swung the pike over his shoulder, turned up his collar and pulled the leather hat down low over his forehead. Now he looked like a regular soldier.

Time crawled by. Sometimes Peter sought brief shelter from the chilling wind in a nook in the castle wall. Turnip-nose didn't return. Good. Everything was going according to plan. The man was certainly giving his tooth a good rinsing.

Peter waited, but he wasn't waiting for Turnip-nose. In the snow near the gate, he had spotted fresh tracks leading out. Had the rider been the black phantom?

Peter paced and waited. At last he heard a distant sound, a sound like far-off hoofbeats in the snow. They were coming closer.

Quickly he stepped back into the shadows of the wall, listening closely. Yes, he was right. The sound of horse's hooves now clattered on the drawbridge. From the other side of the heavy doors came the snorts of a panting horse. Peter was the guard: What did he have to do? How did a soldier act in this situation?

Before he had thought it all out, he jerked open the small hatch in one of the doors and peered out. At the gate stood a horse and rider. The man was dressed in black. From his shoulders hung a long cloak and on his head he wore a broad-rimmed hat. The most striking thing about him, however, was his face. He looked as if he didn't have one. The space below the hat was black except for two pale, piercing eyes that glared at Peter. Peter's first impulse was to slam the hatch and run. But then the black rider barked, "Are the ravens still black?"

"The password!" thought Peter. Impulsively he responded, "Yes, sir, the ravens are still black."

"Then get the lead out and open that door!"

Peter lifted the heavy beam and slid back the huge bolts. The rider trotted into the courtyard. Without a second look at the gatekeeper, the man vaulted from his saddle and tossed the reins to Peter. He hurried toward the castle, his cloak billowing behind him.

Peter watched him go. The black phantom! He had been right. And yet, although ever since last night's talk with Alma, Peter had been expecting him, still, Peter was almost unnerved.

He looked at the horse. He supposed is was the gatekeeper's duty to take care of it. He led it to a stall, unbuckled the saddle and took off the bridle. His own horse was stabled nearby. Oscar seemed to notice that his master was in the vicinity, for he whinnied softly and jerked at his halter. Peter went to him and patted his neck to quiet him down. Seeing that his feedbox was empty, he fetched an armload of fresh hay and spread it in the trough. The black phantom's horse stretched his neck and reached out for the hay with his lips. Peter shrugged. Just because the horse's master had hurled a knife at him was no reason to be cruel to the horse. Peter went back for another armload of hay and filled his feedbox too.

Peter moved very quickly, for time was precious now. He had resolved to crack the mystery of the old mill tonight and it was already very late. He had to hurry while he had the chance. Quickly he left the stable. After surveying the area, he opened the big door that he had bolted behind the black phantom. Without another moment's hesitation, he slipped outside and carefully closed the door behind him.

A thin cloud cover had vanished; now the moonlight was much brighter. The trail of hoofprints leading from the woods to the gate was clearly visible. From last night's outing Peter had learned that at one side of the castle a ridge of trees ran from the woods almost to the moat. Stooping low and using the bank of the moat for cover, he hurried to that side. Taking this route, he ran a lesser chance of being spotted through one of the castle windows. In a quick dash he covered the short open space between the moat and the woods and then melted into the black shadows. After a short search he found the trail of hoofprints again. Since the darkness of the forest made the trail much harder to follow, his progress was slow.

But he didn't give up. At last he heard the sound of rushing water in the distance. Somewhere over there was the creek that led to the old mill. A little later the trail led him to a narrow, rickety bridge. Apparently it was strong enough to bear a horse and rider, for the tracks led straight across it. On the other side they turned to follow the creek downstream.

Peter followed the tracks until they suddenly ended at the foot of a huge spruce tree. Here there was a mish-mash of many hoofprints. Now a set of boot-tracks continued in the snow. Peter surmised what had happened: the man had tied his horse to the tree and gone farther on foot.

Bending low to follow the footprints, Peter continued on. What . . . ? That was weird! The footprints led to the edge of the creek and then vanished. As Peter straightened up and looked across the water, he recoiled with a sudden shock. There loomed the dark, eerie shape of the old mill.

A moment later the astonishment left his face and he almost laughed out loud at his own foolishness. For a moment that dark ruin had almost made him believe in ghosts!

With a quick leap, he landed on a large flat stone that jutted out of the foaming water. The boiling water wet his boots. Another leap put him on a rock right next to the dark, mossy wall of the mill. Resting one hand on a blade of the big wheel, he just managed to keep his balance. Between the wheel and the wall of the mill lay something black. Reaching forward, he discovered what it was: the missing piece of wooden trough that had once brought the water to the top of the water wheel.

Peter looked at the plank wall in front of him. At the height of his shoulders a board was missing. The board beside the opening was fastened by only one nail, and so he could lift it like a hatch. With a small leap, he hoisted himself head-first through this larger opening. Wriggling forward, he soon had his lower body inside too.

He scrambled to his feet and dusted himself off. Straining his eyes, he studied the deep shadows for something unusual, and he listened closely for any sounds of approaching danger. But all he heard was the murmur of the water in the creek.

A cold current of air brushed his cheek. He shuddered, but not with cold. A black shadow silently flitted past his head and two green eyes lit up in the darkness. A gray owl. Peter scolded himself for getting frightened so easily. But he remained alert. It was here that the black phantom had hurled a knife at him two nights ago. True, the mysterious rider had entered the castle not long ago, but Peter had to stay on guard. He had no idea how many people were involved in these strange happenings.

Cautiously he moved forward through the darkness. Before him lay the huge, broken millstone. Again he began to climb the shaky ladder to the loft, nearly falling when he forgot the missing rung. The second story was much lighter than the floor below; moonlight flooded in through the open door.

Peter walked to it and looked down, smiling as he remembered his ridiculous ambush of Alma yesterday. But her disguise would have fooled anyone. She had looked just like the black phantom from up here.

The black phantom . . . How had that mysterious figure appeared in the doorway so suddenly that night? And how had he disappeared so suddenly without leaving any tracks in the snow? Peter leaned forward as far as he could and estimated the distance from the floor below to the sill of the upper opening. He whistled softly through his teeth. It would take a man with strong hands and the body of an acrobat, but it could be done.

When he had come here the first time, the black phantom must have been in the mill, and he had quickly climbed into the loft when he'd heard Peter coming. Then he'd swung down through this opening. That explained his sudden appearance in the doorway. After throwing the knife, he must have jumped up, seized the sill and pulled himself back up into the loft again.

Peter laughed at himself. It was stupid of him not to

have thought of it sooner. The mystery of the missing footprints was solved. But it was only a small part of the bigger mystery: What was the black phantom doing here, and what was happening at the castle? The problems were by no means solved. Maybe he wasn't even getting close. Maybe he'd never find out.

Carefully he climbed back down the wooden ladder.

HE candles of the candelabra on the table had burnt down and flickered out. The smoldering fire in the fireplace gave the only light to the room, a faint red glow touching the walls and ceiling beams. Sometimes the stillness was broken by a snap from the dying coals.

At first glance the room seemed empty, but against the rectangle of the window a silhouette was dimly visible. Alma was sitting motionless in the deep window seat, watching and waiting. Her thoughts dwelt on the events of the past few days. Worry etched lines into her pale forehead, but then they faded. No matter how worried she might be and no matter how threatening the future seemed, she now had a friend. In the middle of this frightening loneliness someone had come to help her—Peter.

She was sitting in the darkness of her room, watching and waiting. When Peter had asked her to keep a sharp lookout, she had promised she would. Below in the castle courtyard, she could just vaguely make out the shape of the guard near the gate. It was Peter, but Alma didn't know that; in the darkness and at this distance she didn't recognize him.

Sometimes the guard stood still and sometimes he paced slowly back and forth. Alma hadn't been sitting there long when, across the moonlit snowfields outside the castle walls, she saw a black figure approaching. As it came closer she saw that it was the black rider. Faintly she heard the horse's hooves thumping across the drawbridge. The guard must have heard him coming and opened the gate, for a few moments later the mysterious rider rode into the courtyard.

Alma thought of Peter and her promise to him. He should know this at once. She slipped out of the window seat and hurried to the door. She would tell him right now. By the dim light of the single torch she hurried down the corridor and found the right door. Good thing that earlier in the day she had checked to see where Peter's room was. She knocked, and when she got no immediate answer, she opened the door and stepped inside.

Darkness! The room was completely dark. That startled her. The fire was dead on the hearth. By the moonlight that fell through the window, she could see that the big chair was empty.

She took a few steps into the room, and her own voice frightened her as she whispered, "Peter!"

The darkness didn't answer.

"Peter!" she whispered again, more urgently this time.

But she got no answer. Along one wall of the room was the dark shape of a canopy bed. The curtains were pulled closed. Alma quickly stepped toward it. Was Peter asleep? No doubt. Everyone should be sleeping at this time of the night. She pulled the curtain aside and reached into the darkness to shake Peter awake.

The next instant she pulled back her hand as if it had

been burned. With all her willpower, she fought back a scream. For a moment she stared, eyes wide with horror, into the shadows between the curtains. Then she turned and fled toward the door. Dry sobs welled up in her throat and she gasped for air.

Flying into her own room, she threw herself onto her bed and pushed her face into her pillow, trying to blot the scene out of her mind. Who was that in Peter's bed? It certainly wasn't Peter! She shuddered; her mind felt numb. When she had reached in to shake Peter awake, her hand had touched a face. But what a face! A fat, flabby face with a greasy rag tied around it. And her fingers had touched a long, wet moustache.

Was someone else sleeping in Peter's bed? Where was Peter? Was he . . . ? A dreadful suspicion crept into her heart. Was Peter the friend he had claimed to be? Should she trust him as completely, as willingly as she had done? With a violent shake of her head, she tried to put the doubts out of her head. Perhaps he was out on one of his clue-hunting excursions. But . . . but what was that strange man doing in his bed? Again suspicions assaulted her mind. Tears burned in her eyes.

At the edge of the woods, Peter stopped to study the black silhouette of the castle. He was worried. Had he closed the castle gate behind him or not? His sleepless night and the long trip to the old mill through darkness and deep snow had drained him.

When he reached the drawbridge, he tiptoed across and carefully pushed the huge door. He scowled. The big door was locked. Someone must have bolted the door after he had left. That might mean that he had been discovered! Had Turnip-nose returned, or had

someone else found the gate loose and fastened it?
Carefully he pushed against the little hatch in the door.
It opened. When he peered in, to his relief he saw the
dark shape of Turnip-nose on the other side. Apparently
the man had heard the little hatch squeak, for he turned
and hurried to the gate.

Quickly Peter searched his mind for a likely story. He
had promised Turnip-nose to keep watch for him while
he rinsed his tooth, but he had been gone for who knows
how long. Well, Turnip-nose didn't know who he was;
he'd just keep playing his mysterious role.

"Are the ravens still black?" he whispered through
the hole.

Turnip-nose answered at once: "Yes, sir, the ravens
are still black."

Immediately he unlocked the gate to let Peter in. He
looked so guilty that Peter knew that he had nothing to
fear from him. Turnip-nose swayed from side to side.
He had rinsed his tooth pretty thoroughly. Peter
wondered whether he had emptied the whole jug.

"Hello, my good fellow, it looks like your tooth is
feeling better," said Peter, as he handed back the cloak
and leather hat. "I went to the edge of the woods to investigate. I thought I heard strange sounds out there.
But I didn't see anything."

As he spoke, he started toward the castle without
giving the unsettled but obviously relieved soldier any
chance to ask questions. A few minutes later he was lying in his bed. But sleep didn't come. Too many things
crowded in on his mind.

The next morning when Turnip-nose set Peter's silver
breakfast tray on the table, Peter was already up and

dressed. As he sat down, he asked Turnip-nose how his tooth was doing. His next question was meant to needle the man a little. "I suppose it took a little while before the rinsing began to do any good, eh?"

Turnip-nose swallowed.

"It was quite a while before you got back," continued Peter.

Secretly Peter enjoyed the alarmed expression on the man's face. The first thing he had done this morning was to look into the wine pitcher on the table. As he had suspected, it was empty. No wonder Turnip-nose hadn't returned right away.

Peter did not know, however, that the wine had made the man so sleepy that he had stretched out on Peter's bed—only for a moment, of course. But immediately he had dropped off into a deep sleep. He probably wouldn't have woke up until this morning if a hand hadn't groped over his face and his wine-drenched moustache. He had bolted up in fright.

At first he hadn't known where he was, and when he had pushed aside the canopy curtain, he had glimpsed a pale figure flit out through the door. With a shock he had realized that he had been sleeping in Master Peter's bed, and he had hurried out of the castle to his post at the gate. When he got there, Master Peter had been gone and the gate had been standing ajar. After closing the gate, he had taken his post again, but without his cloak and hat. And it had been cold.

As he ate his breakfast, Peter acted as if all his attention was fixed on his food, but he kept a close eye on his attendant. Turnip-nose obviously considered him one of the gang. The simple man seemed to have forgotten any

uncertainties he may have had about last night. He was
in a good mood this morning, for after telling Peter that
the countess again wished to speak to him, he said in a
gloating, confiding voice, "Things are going good,
aren't they? We're going to make a big haul, I hear."

Peter almost choked on his food. A big haul! Once
again it sounded like the black raven was the sign of a
gang of thieves! But he still didn't know where they
planned to strike. Perhaps he could learn more.

"Yes," he said in the same confidential tone that
Turnip-nose had used. "Yes, things look good. But we
mustn't count our chickens before they hatch. You're
not really sure until the booty is in your hands, I always
say."

Turnip-nose looked a bit crestfallen. "But . . . but I
thought the booty had already been brought to the
boats?"

Peter almost betrayed himself this time. So that was
what they were after! With some effort, he maintained
his poise. The booty was on the boats! The gang was
after the goods that had been collected from the farmers
for rent. And he was going to pay for those goods! So
the thieves had their eyes on a double haul.

His mouth full of food, Peter mumbled, "Yes, that's
true, but anything can happen."

Frowning thoughtfully Turnip-nose stoked up the fire
in the fireplace.

That same morning Alma opened the door of her
room and looked down the corridor. When she saw no
one, she hurried toward Peter's door. She knew that
after her horrible fright she wouldn't have any peace of
mind until she found out who had been sleeping in

Peter's bed. The only way to find out, she had decided, was to tell the whole story to Peter and see how he reacted. So she was eager to talk to him as soon as she could.

That night it had seemed as though a little demon had sat on her pillow, and every time she had almost fallen asleep, he had shaken her awake to hiss in her ear, "Are you sure he's a friend? Maybe it was all an act. Is he really as honest as he looks? Perhaps he's playing you for a fool."

The little demon had aroused fear and distrust in her heart. Angrily she had kept trying to shake those nasty thoughts from her mind. After all, it was quite possible that Peter had been out investigating all those mysterious happenings. But then how did that awful man with the sticky moustache get into his bed? As she thought of how she had put her hand on that disgusting face, a shiver went down her back.

Ahead was Peter's door. Now she would ask him. She had confided in him; now he would have to tell her where he had been last night. She raised her hand to knock, but lowered it again. Did Peter have a visitor? Who could it be at this hour? She didn't want to interrupt. Hesitating, she wondered whether it wouldn't be better to come back later when he was alone.

Although she didn't mean to eavesdrop, suddenly she picked up some of the conversation behind the closed door. She turned pale.

A voice said, "We're going to make a big haul, I hear." Another voice answered, a voice she recognized as Peter's, "Yes, things look good. But we mustn't count our chickens before they hatch. You're not really sure until the booty is in your hands, I always say."

The words were like an icy hand clutching her heart.

For a second she stared, horrified, at the closed door, and then she whirled and fled, dry sobs welling up in her chest.

Dashing into her room, she threw herself onto the bed and wept into her pillow. Why had he tricked her? Why had she believed him?

She still found it hard to believe. He had seemed so honest. They had shared such a friendly talk, and she had been sure he was an ally. Why, oh, why had she been so foolish as to confide in a total stranger? If only she had never met him! Maybe he was to blame for all the awful things that were happening around here.

When Peter had finished his breakfast, he rose to go to his meeting with the countess. Turnip-nose had already left the room. Peter frowned. "We're going to make a big haul." If he continued to work on this business alone, he was asking for trouble. This time he would tell the countess what he had learned. Perhaps she could tell him more, and by putting their heads together they'd be able to solve the mystery. Yes, it was his duty to tell her what was happening in her castle.

At the door of the castle hall, the guard told him that the countess had just arrived. He knocked and opened the door for Peter.

The old woman received him with her customary courtesy. She pointed to the chair where he had sat before. Peter wanted to speak what was on his mind at once, but he couldn't. The oily, bearded dandy was in the room. His presence frustrated Peter; now he felt that he had to weigh every word carefully. The servant undoubtedly played some role in the shady things happening at the castle. But what kind of a role?

Dandy Dan sat at a table near a window and didn't look up as he dipped his quill and kept writing. However, Peter was sure that the man was listening carefully to every word they spoke.

The countess didn't give Peter much time to think. She got right down to business. Now that her men had hauled the last load onto the ships, the time had come to close the deal. They quickly agreed on the price Peter would pay for all the goods. Peter hesitated. Should he hand over such a huge amount to the countess? Was it safe to do so in the presence of that repulsive man with the prying eyes? If only he weren't here! The countess should know about the dangers he had discovered. Peter resolved to speak to her again as soon as possible—but privately.Where could he do that, however? All the walls and doors in this castle seemed to have eyes and ears . . . Alma! She could help. He would try to find her after he left the countess.

Peter took out his purse, feeling he had no choice. As he counted out the countess's money, Peter felt Dandy Dan counting along from his corner of the room. The countess told him that she had arranged to have the ships depart early the following morning. "If you wish to sail home aboard one of the ships, the captain will be happy to accommodate you."

Peter thought fast. For a second he had the impulse to spill everything, to shout, "You are being deceived! Evil men in your service have other plans for those ships. They'll probably sail in the opposite direction."

But because of Dandy Dan's presence, all he said was, "I'd love to go along, but I'd better return by horseback so that I can arrange for the goods to be unloaded."

Peter rose from his chair. At a motion from the countess, Dandy Dan sprang up from his table to lead him out. At the door Peter turned and, as was the custom, bowed deeply toward the countess.

Again Dandy Dan led him through the corridor to his own door. After opening the door for Peter, he stepped back and made a slight bow. Again Peter sensed that the bow, outwardly a sign of polite submission, was actually the opposite, for the man's dark eyes flickered with contempt and mockery.

Peter clenched his fist. What if he grabbed the man by the collar, hurled him into the room, slammed the door behind them, and shook some answers out of this fellow? Peter would have loved to change the expression on that oily face, with his fists if need be. But he fought down the impulse—not because he was afraid, but because he thought he might lose more by it than he would gain. Ignoring the man's little smirk, he stepped inside and slammed the door behind him before Dandy Dan could touch it.

ETER took several steps into the room. Then he paused and listened to be sure the valet returned to the hall. Out in the corridor footsteps retreated from his door. Briefly he considered what to do next. His first thought was to go to Alma's room and arrange somehow to reach her grandmother when the old woman was alone. But another thing, more pressing at the moment, occupied his mind. He had to know whether Thune had been able to deliver his letter in time for the mail coach.

Peter made up his mind. Grabbing his fur coat, he hurried to the courtyard to saddle his horse. The guard at the gate opened the big door for him and Oscar's hooves clattered onto the drawbridge. The sun was shining, but snow clouds were gathering over the woods. He chose the road leading around the woods rather than one cutting through them.

He reached Thune's cabin and banged on the door. His eyebrows rose quizzically as a deep growl sounded on the other side of the door. The growling quickly became loud barking. A dog? Strange, he'd never seen Thune with a dog before. Peter waited as Thune calmed the dog with a few firm words. The bolts squeaked, and Thune opened the door a crack to peer outside. When he saw Peter standing in the snow, his face broke into an eager smile. Holding the dog by the scruff of the neck, he fumbled with the chain and let Peter in. The dog sniffed suspiciously at Peter's boots, but apparently satisfied that Peter posed no threat, he padded back to his place beside the crackling fireplace.

In a gush of angry words Thune told Peter what he had found when he arrived home late last night. The door to his shed had been broken to pieces and someone had made off with his whole store of grain and furs. Peter tried to calm him down so that he could ask some questions. When Thune had vented his rage somewhat, Peter asked him whether he had arrived at the tollhouse in time.

"Yes," answered Thune. "With my own eyes I saw the letter put aboard the coach."

Peter sat down at the table, nodding his head in satisfaction. "Where did you get the dog?" he asked, pointing to the dog at the fireplace.

Thune described how he had come upon the dog in the middle of the woods, and he also told Peter about the boot it had been carrying. "See, there it is."

"Where?"

"Under the dog. He's lying on it. That dog followed me all the way home, and he lugged that boot the whole way."

With a start, Peter took another look at the dog. That dog . . . ? Was it possible? He too had run into a dog recently. Only two nights ago. In the dark. He had almost forgotten, but now he recalled the scare it had given him as he was leaving by the back gate of the castle. A dog had brushed past his legs and flitted into the woods. Was this shaggy beast lying in front of the fireplace the same one he had seen then? It was possible. Too bad it had been so dark. He wouldn't be able to recognize the dog if he saw him.

Thune bent down and pulled the boot out from under the dog. The animal growled softly but didn't get up. However, he kept a close eye on the boot as Thune showed it to Peter. It was a very tall boot cut to fit over the knee. The top edge was folded down.

"Why do you think that dog hangs on to this thing all the time?" asked Thune.

Peter thought aloud, "Maybe the dog lost its master and found his boot in the woods. But how could someone lose a boot like this?"

"Yeah," said Thune, "that's the first question that came to my mind too. It's strange."

Peter wasn't listening. A sudden image had flashed into his mind. Once again he saw the wagon loaded with branches. Had it been a boot sticking out of the back after all? And was this that boot? It all seemed so far-fetched, but everything that had been happening lately was improbable. Even the most unlikely things were beginning to seem likely.

Peter stood up. It was high time for him to get back to the castle. Many things still had to be done. First he had to talk to Alma. And then to Alma's grandmother. He thanked Thune for delivering his letter for him and showed his appreciation with a generous gift.

As he mounted his horse to ride off, Peter heard Thune carefully bolt the door behind him and then fasten the chain. He grinned to himself. In a way he couldn't blame the man, living all by himself on the edge of the woods where all these strange things happened. Thune had become especially fearful since the night Peter had slept over and he had found the dead raven hanging over his door.

What was all this mysterious hocus-pocus with ravens?

First a dead raven over Thune's door.

Then a raven on the handle of the knife that had been hurled at him.

Then the wagon driver with a real raven on his shoulder.

And the password Turnip-nose had given him: "Are the ravens still black?"

Suddenly a light flashed on. Password? Was it merely a password? He had learned that the right answer was, "Yes, the ravens are still black." The words were no doubt used as a sign of recognition by a group of men with evil intentions. But it could also be a code to tell one another that everything was safe. If their plans were threatened or something was amiss, they could answer, "No, the ravens aren't black." And a raven that isn't black is a gray raven.

At this thought, Peter reined in his horse and stopped. Did it fit? Yes, why not? It not only seemed possible, it seemed probably. He turned in his saddle. Thune's cabin was still in sight. Quickly he turned his horse back to the house. Thune didn't come out when he dismounted beside the shed. He probably hadn't noticed that Peter had come back. That was fine with Peter. He would have had trouble explaining what he was about to do. In fact, he didn't really know himself why he was doing this. He kicked through the snow beside the shed where Thune had tossed the dead raven. It didn't take him long to find it. A plan had formed in his mind. Would it work? He shrugged. All he could do was try. No better ideas had come to him.

That first night the black phantom must have followed Peter's trail as he left the mill to return to Thune's cabin. Perhaps he had hung the dead raven—a gray one—on the door as a warning to other members of the gang. A gray raven meant, Beware! Danger!

But how had the black phantom found a gray raven so quickly? There were still many loose ends in his theory. On the other hand, there were plenty of ravens, gray and black, in these woods. To shoot one down was no problem for a good marksman. It would have been done at first light of day. Peter couldn't come up with a better explanation.

In any case, now it was his turn. He had the gray raven, and now he would give the black phantom a taste of his own medicine. He mounted his horse again. This time, however, he took the path that led through the woods past the mill. When he reached the clearing around the mill, he rode across it and right up to the door. Taking out the dead raven, he hung it from a nail that stuck out above the door. As he rode off, he looked back. It was a strange sight, that grisly thing hanging over the doorway. Peter wasn't really sure why he had done it, and he had no idea what kind of results it would have. If any.

Peter loitered in the castle courtyard, not knowing what to do. It was afternoon. After returning from Thune's place, he immediately had tried to see Alma. He had knocked on her door, quietly and politely at

first, and then harder. But he'd gotten no response.
Carefully testing the doorknob, he had found it locked.
She must have gone. But where? After dinner, he had
tried to see the countess. The guard who was always
posted at her door told him that the countess was not in
the hall and that she never saw anyone in the afternoon.

Now he was hanging about in the courtyard with
nothing to do but wait. He had wandered over to the
stable once to check Oscar's leg. Should he take his
horse to the village blacksmith? He looked up at the sky.
It was too late now; soon the sun would begin to set.
Turnip-nose had told him that the castle blacksmith
could shoe his horse. But the man was gone, and he
wouldn't be back until tomorrow or the next day. He
was working at the ships with other men from the castle.

Bored, his hands tucked inside his fur coat, Peter
watched two stablehands drag hay from the haystack to
the stables. He strolled past the drawbridge that led to
the castle entrance. The water of the inner moat was
covered with a thin layer of ice. He looked up at the
walls towering above the water. One of the windows
directly overhead was Alma's. Where had she gone and
why was she staying away so long? About half an hour
ago he had tried her door again, but it had been still
locked. Had she discovered anything new?

The sun slowly sank toward the horizon dropping
behind the high castle walls. The courtyard was cast in
shadow, but the last light painted the castle's sloping
roofs and towers a deep crimson. The windows flashed
like fire in the sun. Peter sauntered to the side of the castle. Tomorrow he would have to leave for home. But
how could he go before he had solved the mystery of the
black raven gang and before he had settled accounts
with the black phantom? Soon he would check once

more to see if Alma had returned to her room. It wasn't just for his own sake that he had resolved to get to the bottom of these mysterious events. He had promised her he would.

Suddenly he ducked behind the open door of a shed. He had hidden instinctively. Had the man seen him already? He put an eye to the crack between the wall and the door. Over there was the small gate that led to the woods. The man stood at the gate, holding his horse's reins in one hand, while with the other he slid back the bolt that locked the gate. When the man cast a hurried glance around as if he were afraid to be seen, Peter saw who he was: the man with the pointed beard—Dandy Dan! Where was he going, and why was he acting so secretive?

The man disappeared through the gate, carefully closing it behind him. Peter ground his teeth in frustration, but not because the man was leaving. No, he'd just as soon never set eyes on that dandy again. He was frustrated because his own horse was lame, and that meant he couldn't follow the man. And he was convinced that if he found out where Dandy Dan was going and what he was up to, many of his questions would be answered. Peter clenched his fists in chagrin, but there was nothing he could do. At last he just shrugged his shoulders and tried to forget it.

Darkness had fallen. After the sun had set in a blaze of red and violet, dark clouds had come surging in from the river like black pirate ships. A piercing east wind now drove stinging sheets of fine snow across the fields.

Down in the village the wind rattled the locked shutters of the inn. Angrily it packed snow into the corners of the window sills and against the low door. Whirling around the feedboxes and the old linden tree, it sculpted ragged snowdrifts. Inside the inn behind the closed shutters, the oil lamp flickered as the wind howled in the big chimney, making the fire in the fireplace flare up in sudden gusts. Several farmers sat near the fireplace sunk in somber thought. The rosy glow of the flames danced over their weathered faces. Quietly, bitterly, they stared into the flames. No one said a word. Everything had already been said. What they had feared had finally happened.

They had lost everything. Everything they had worked hard for all year had been stolen from them. It had all been hauled away to the ships on the river, and what could they do about it? Nothing! The strange, savage soldiers from the castle had laughed at them while the farmers had looked on helplessly with clenched fists.

And now . . . ? What now? What would happen to them now? To their families? That worry etched deep lines into their foreheads touched by the glow of firelight. That question drew their lips into thin, hard lines and that darkened their eyes with despair.

Crash! Suddenly the inn door flew wide open. A blast of stinging snow whipped into the room, extinguishing the oil lamp. The men shuddered with cold, and turned, startled, toward the door. What was this? Someone stepped into the darkened room and slammed the door shut again.

The innkeeper snatched a coal from the fireplace, relit the lamp, and lifted it high. The yellow glow of the lamp fell on the figure of a girl. Panting, she leaned back

against the door. Her long cloak was coated with snow. She threw back the hood from her head and shook out her long, blond hair.

The innkeeper's hand shook in consternation, and the farmers stared at the girl open-mouthed. This was the young lady from the castle—the countess's grand-daughter! What was she doing here? Here, in this inn for peasant farmers, and in this foul weather, and all alone? The men weren't left guessing long; the girl took a couple of steps forward and began to speak.

It was an incredible, confused story. The men listened with growing wonder which gradually became angry outrage. Yes, they knew the man she was talking about—that fancy young merchant.

One of the men slammed his fist on the table in rage. "That silver-tongued villain!"

The innkeeper was still holding the oil lamp. He had forgotten to lower his arm. He had also forgotten to close his mouth, which still gaped at the young woman.

Suddenly all the farmers erupted at once, shouting angrily.

"He was sitting at this very table not a week ago! That wolf!"

"That's right, and he went home with Thune."

"Thune? Yes, where is Thune, anyway? He put him up for the night."

"How come Thune isn't here?"

"That's funny. Thune is always here. I hear he's pretty thick with that four-flusher."

"Do you suppose he was taken in by that swindler, that cheat, that thief?"

"Let's hang him! He'd let us and our families starve. Let's hang him and take back our grain and furs!"

The farmers had stood up and several of them,

flushed with rage, started toward the door. One of them, however, sprang forward and, holding up his hands, shouted over the noise. "Wait a minute, men! Wait a minute! Calm down! This isn't the way to do it!"

The clamor subsided for a moment.

"Listen, men, let's not go running off half-cocked. We've got to stick together. We've got to make a plan. That fellow isn't alone. Those new so-called soldiers at the castle are working for him. We don't have a chance if we don't go as a group."

"He's right!" one man chimed in.

"We better arm ourselves," said another.

No one paid any further attention to Alma. She had not foreseen this violent outburst of anger. Frightened by all the ranting and fury, she retreated to the wall.

She had spent the day locked in her room. After overhearing Peter's conversation, she had run back to her own room and locked the door. Throwing herself on her bed, she had cried herself to sleep. Had someone knocked at her door and tried the doorknob? Or had she merely dreamt it? She wasn't sure. Was the castle occupied by robbers? And was her grandmother a prisoner? Not knowing where else to turn, Alma had finally decided to go to the village and ask the farmers for help. The kitchen girl had helped her sneak a horse out through the back gate.

But now? The farmers had gone wild with rage. She hadn't expected this. Had they been robbed too? She looked on in terror and confusion. What would happen now? A few minutes later some of the farmers were already beginning to return, carrying torches, pitchforks, pikes, axes, and flails. Most of them were mounted. Soon the shouts of angry men had become the rumble of a mob seeking its own justice.

FTER loitering about the courtyard until dark, Peter returned to his room. Without much hope, he knocked on Alma's door once again. No one answered and the door remained locked.

Disappointed, he withdrew to his own room. He felt cold. Shivering, he poked up the fire in the fireplace. After pulling off his boots, he sat down at a corner of the table and examined the knife with the black raven on the handle. He stared hard at the handle as if by staring hard enough he could discover its secret. He took a piece of wood from the woodbox and began hacking at it, lost in thought. All at once he saw that he had begun to carve the piece of wood into the shape of a bird. With a little imagination it looked like a sitting raven.

A welter of thoughts swarmed through Peter's mind, but one image kept coming to the fore—the image of a girl with golden hair. The night when he had talked with Alma in her room, he had seen in her eyes trust and an appeal for help—not just for herself, but also for her grandmother. Full of warmth and concern, he had sworn to live up to that trust.

113

Now, however, he felt himself sinking into a quagmire of guesses and uncertainties. Would he ever solve all these puzzles? Questions kept flashing through his mind. Who was the black apparition? What was he doing at the old mill at midnight? What caused that pitiful wailing? Was it a human sound? If it was, what kind of human being could utter such an eerie, chilling cry? No normal person would make a sound like that. Where did the black apparition hide during the day? Here at the castle?

Peter's knife paused as he considered this possibility. Perhaps the black apparition didn't hide. Perhaps he went about his business just as Peter did. Could he be the valet with the pointed beard—the one he called Dandy Dan? Yes, it was possible, but he could also be almost anyone else in the castle. Was it the wagon driver with the raven? But Peter had seen him at the castle only once. Since the night Peter had ducked into Alma's room, he hadn't seen the man again.

Why had the wagon driver been headed toward the swamp that first day? More and more Peter suspected that he hadn't been hauling just branches. But what had he been hauling? And where was that man now? Unable to find any answers, Peter felt discouraged and also angry. With a vicious slash he cut the head off of the raven he had been carving. Peter watched the head roll across the floor. Suddenly he stared hard.

The wooden head had come to rest beside his boots. Slowly the gloomy scowl disappeared from Peter's face and was replaced by a look of eager wonderment. Was it possible? Had he stumbled upon the clue that would solve the mystery?

On the floor beside his boot lay a small puddle of water. This was nothing unusual. Snow had been caked on his boots and the heat of the fire had melted it. However, this puddle reminded him of a similar puddle he had seen earlier today.

That morning when he had said goodbye to the countess and had made his deep bow at the door, he had seen a similar puddle right in front of him and in the shape of a footprint. At the time he had thought nothing of it, but now he realized that it meant that someone had been in the hall before him—someone who had come from outside.

That person must have come in some time earlier; otherwise the snow would not have had time to melt in the cold hall. And the footprint must have been made early that morning, because if it had been made the night before, the water certainly would have dried up.

After returning to the castle early this morning, had the black phantom been in the hall? Did the countess know what was going on? It was his duty to inform her and to help her plan what to do.

Peter had made up his mind. He would go to the countess and tell her everything he knew. He buckled on his sword, stuck the raven-knife in his belt, and pulled on his boots. The corridor was dark and quiet. To Peter's surprise, there was no guard at the door to the main hall. Was the countess not here? Now what would he do? Where should he look for her? The door to the hall stood slightly ajar, and the room beyond was dark. Pushing the door a little further open, Peter stuck his head inside to take a last quick look. He started.

The countess *was* in the room! But she didn't see Peter because she was looking out of one of the tall windows. Her bowed and weary figure was silhouetted against the lighter window.

Peter was about to withdraw his head when he saw that she was holding a candelabrum with several burning candles. She lifted it high over her head and then lowered it to the sill. She repeated this motion several times. From where he stood, Peter could see past the old woman's shoulder into the darkness beyond. Far away in the dark fields another light twinkled. It, too, moved up and down.

Peter blinked in disbelief. The countess was standing at the window signaling to someone outside. He started to pull back his head to think over what he had just seen. As he did so, he bumped the door with his elbow.

Startled by the sudden noise behind her, the countess whirled. With her free hand she quickly pulled the veil down over her face, for it had been folded back. But she was too late to prevent Peter from glimpsing her angular profile against the window. Spotting Peter in the doorway, she quickly set the candelabrum on the sill and snatched up her cane. Before Peter realized what was happening, she had twisted the cane handle and pulled it free. Peter's eye caught the glint of cold steel. The cane must have been hollow, for she was suddenly holding a short sword.

For a moment Peter stood in the doorway, stunned. Was he being attacked? Who was this standing before him with a drawn sword? Was it the old countess? No, it couldn't be. That angular profile he had seen against the window was a man's profile. Well, Peter wasn't going to let himself be frightened off. He drew his own sword and took two quick steps into the room. As the countess's blade lunged toward his chest, he parried it with his own.

A fierce battle ensued. In the dark and unfamiliar room, Peter crashed into a chair. His sword struck the edge of a table and clattered out of his hand. Wheeling, he grabbed the back of the chair and hurled it at his opponent. The impact knocked the cane-sword out of the countess's hand, and it skidded across the stone floor. One leg of the chair caught the countess's veil and jerked it off her head. Now Peter found himself face to face with a man—as he had suspected.

Peter had never seen this face before, but he had no time to stand there gawking. The man lunged at him, catching him around the waist. Peter hurtled backwards over the table and crashed to the floor on the other side. Scrambling up, he sprang forward, shoving the table ahead of him, trying to ram his opponent into a corner. The man was no weakling, however. Peter's muscles quivered in this match of strength against strength as they strained in opposite directions. The man now had an advantage, for his back was against the wall. He managed to bring up his foot behind the table, and then, with a sudden thrust, he catapulted Peter and the table across the room.

As Peter scrambled to his feet, the man attacked, fists flailing. Peter ducked and counter-punched. Suddenly Peter heard wild screeching just behind him. A high-backed armchair which had been covered by a cloth had been knocked over. From under the cloth burst a large black bird—a raven. Peter's opponent took advantage of this momentary distraction to snatch up the heavy silver candelabrum on the windowsill. The next instant Peter caught a bone-jarring blow to the head. Bright lights exploded behind his eyes and he felt himself falling, falling into a deep hole that seemed to have opened in the floor. His head spun and the darkness threatened to swallow him.

The thought flashed through Peter's mind, "I've lost. It's all over." But he wouldn't accept defeat. He struggled to shake off the blinding numbness. In a dim fog he saw the shadow of his enemy against the gray rectangle of the window. In one upraised hand, he held the heavy candelabrum.

Drawing on his last ounces of strength, Peter coiled himself like a spring and lunged. His head struck his opponent like a battering ram in his exposed midsection. Caught off balance by the unexpected attack, the man staggered backward, his arms flailing. The long skirts slapped Peter's face as Peter crashed to the floor. Peter heard the sound of breaking glass and then a muffled splash. He couldn't get up, and again darkness closed in on him. A trickle of blood ran down his forehead into one eye, but Peter didn't notice.

LOWLY Peter opened his eyes. His head throbbed painfully. "I lost, I lost!" The refrain hammered through his head. "I let that raven distract me. How stupid of me! It's all my fault. I failed!"

What now? Peter looked about him. He was still lying amid the wreckage of the castle hall. Strange that the man had left him lying here. He half expected to be waking up in one of the dungeons of the castle. Rather than try to get up, Peter remained where he was for a few more moments, trying to collect his thoughts. His hand found a painful bruise on his scalp. The blood was beginning to crust in his hair.

Where was his opponent and where was that blasted raven? Painfully he pulled himself up, using the table as a crutch. Then he saw the tall windows. One of them was smashed—completely knocked out. A cold wind blew into the room. Peter stumbled toward it and looked out. Despite his throbbing head, he smiled. Although it was dark, directly below the window in the snow-covered ice of the moat he could see a black, jagged hole.

119

He hadn't lost!

The moat wasn't very wide and a jagged trail had been broken through the ice to the bank. Incredible! His opponent had crashed through the window, fallen more than ten meters, and crashed through the ice below. And then he had still had the strength to break through the ice to get to shore. In the snow, a trail of dark footsteps led away from the moat and disappeared around the corner of the castle. Peter couldn't help but feel some admiration for his enemy.

But where was he now? Would he flee? Or were all the castle guards part of the gang? Then he would have returned to the castle. Then he, Peter, was in great danger! Quickly he retrieved his sword and hurried toward the door. There was no one in the corridor, but as he started toward his room, two men appeared around the corner. For a moment Peter thought that they had come to take him prisoner, but the next moment he realized that they had just happened to be there. They eyed him with surprise and suspicion. All at once he understood their suspicion, and he could have kicked himself for his stupidity. In his hurry he had forgotten to sheath his sword. Had he remembered to do so, he probably would have been able to pass them without any trouble. Now it was too late.

With a shock Peter recognized one of the men—the tall one with the red hair and grim face. It was the wagon driver who had lent him the knife. Peter had wondered briefly whether the man disguised as the countess had been the wagon driver. But no, the man couldn't have returned this quickly; certainly not with dry clothes.

The man cast a quick glance into the castle hall. Seeing the broken window and the overturned furniture, he sprang forward, drawing his sword. "Get him!" he shouted.

Peter prepared to defend himself, but as he sized up his opponents, he saw that he was in deep trouble. The men advanced, brandishing their swords. The tall corridor was suddenly filled with the clash and clatter of swords; the torchlight cast frenzied, darting shadows on the walls. Slowly Peter was driven back toward the stairs leading to the cellar. With a quick thrust, Peter wounded one of the men just above the knee. The man crumpled, momentarily blocking his companion's way. Peter seized the moment to turn and bound down the stairs.

On his left he saw a dark opening. Was it a doorway to the cellar? Stone steps led downward. Trusting to luck, he hurried down until he bumped into a heavy wooden door. Fortunately it opened when he lifted the latch. The space beyond it was totally dark. Quickly he slammed the door behind him, grasped his sword between his teeth, and groped along the edge of the door. His hands trembled as they ran over the rough wood. But at last he found what he was looking for—a bolt. He slid it home just in the nick of time.

The next instant someone was shouting on the other side and hammering on the door. Leaning against the wall, Peter waited to see what would happen. Abruptly the hollering and hammering stopped. Peter could hear only muffled, unintelligible whispers. Then he heard the bolts on the other side of the door being slid into place, followed by the sound of retreating footsteps.

Peter was gripped by fear. Had he locked himself in? Scowling into the darkness, he sheathed his sword.

After staring into the darkness for a while, he thought he detected a spot of light in the distance. Holding his hands out before him, he edged forward step by step. As he drew closer he saw a sizeable window, open and unbarred. His heart began to beat faster. Perhaps all was not lost after all. Looking through the opening, he saw the underside of the drawbridge that spanned the inner moat. Between the moat and the window ran a narrow ledge of stone. Too bad the ice wasn't strong enough to allow him to cross the moat under the bridge.

As he began to climb out, he heard the shuffle of boots and whispering on the bridge directly overhead. Were the men who had chased him waiting for him on the bridge? Did they know about the window, and were they planning to ambush him? If so, he was caught like a mouse in a trap. Peter flattened himself against the wall beside the window. He gritted his teeth. They didn't have him yet. He'd fight for his life.

Peter's suspicions proved correct. He saw a man lower himself from the bridge to the narrow ledge that led to the window. What should he do now? Peter dropped to his haunches, and in the darkness he groped about on the floor. A minute ago his foot had stubbed on something hard. Where was it? He felt panic rising. Aha, his fingers touched something—a short piece of wood. Perhaps it was the beam used to bar the window after the wooden hatch was put in place. But there was no time to grope around for the hatch. Peter picked up the beam and clutched it tightly.

When he returned to the window, he saw that more men were lowering themselves onto the ledge. Just outside the window someone whispered commands to the others. No doubt he was the leader. Was it the red-bearded wagon driver? His voice sounded familiar. The man did not seem to realize that Peter might be standing close enough to hear every word.

"Listen men, I'll go in first and then the rest of you follow me. One at a time and no crowding. When I'm inside, I'll whisper 'Okay' to signal the next man, and he'll signal the next one, and so on. Understood? He's a dangerous enemy so we don't want him to know we're here until we're all inside. All right, here I go!"

Peter grinned humorlessly. Yes, the man was right: he was dangerous—dangerous as only a trapped man can be. He was dangerous because he was desperate.

As the window darkened, he lifted the beam high. The shape of a head and shoulders appeared in the window. Even in the darkness Peter recognized the long neck and bony head. It was the wagon driver. Inside the cellar the man sat hunched on the floor, apparently listening for danger. Peter, standing almost beside him, held his breath and tightened his grip on the raised piece of wood. The wagon driver turned his head and whispered, "Okay!"

Thump!

Peter landed a quick, hard blow on the wagon driver's head. The man uttered a sigh and crumpled to the floor. Peter trembled with suspense. Was he going to get away with it? The next man climbed through the low window. Because of the darkness he didn't see his leader stretched out on the floor.

Thump!

A muffled sound, as though the man hiccupped, and then he too pitched forward. He didn't fall hard because the first man cushioned his fall.

Silently Peter berated himself. He had goofed! The fellow had not had time to signal the next man. But Peter didn't lose his head. Stooping toward the window, he hissed, "Okay."

At once the next man appeared in the opening.

Thump!

"Okay," whispered Peter.

Here came number four.

Thump!

"Okay."

Thump!

"Okay."

Thump!

That was number six.

Thump! Again and again Peter swung his club, losing count in his excitement. Another shadow appeared in the window. What a strange head—so large! Again he swung his club.

An outraged howl sounded outside, followed by angry curses. The shadow was gone. Quickly Peter tossed his club aside, for he had immediately perceived his mistake. With a desperate lunge, he dove through the window. Now he would have to depend on his sword to fight his way out.

But when he looked outside, Peter saw that only one man was left. Fortunately he had made his mistake on the last man. In the darkness of the bridge the man was no more than a silhouette, but Peter recognized him by the two rabbit ears on the top of his head. It was Turnip-nose, and he was holding the seat of his pants with both hands. The stupid man had tried to climb through the window seat-first. Instead of getting a rap on the head, the man had caught the blow on his posterior.

When he spotted Peter emerging from the window, Turnip-nose sprang forward. But Peter was ready and met him with a wicked blow to the chin that sent a searing pain through Peter's fist. That one blow was enough. Slowly Turnip-nose collapsed against the wall.

Now Peter stood alone. He had to act fast, for the heap of men in the cellar might begin to revive at any time. On the outside of the window was a hinged shutter. Peter closed it and fastened it with an iron pin that hung on a small chain.

Stepping over Turnip-nose, Peter started along the ledge. But then he flattened himself in the shadows. Running footsteps sounded overhead, and someone was shouting. Would there be swordplay after all? More voices sounded. Someone was yelling orders. "We're under attack! Enemy at the gate!"

Peter started in surprise. Enemy at the gate? What did that mean? He heard no more footsteps on the bridge. With a quick jump Peter caught hold of the edge of the bridge and swung himself up. Soldiers carrying pikes were running all over the courtyard, but no one paid any attention to him. A yellow glow lit up the towers flanking the main gate. Where was that light coming from? Was there a fire outside the gate? A rumble of angry voices was coming from outside the castle walls. Suddenly he realized what the glow on the towers meant. A mob of angry men carrying torches was at the gate. Who were they? What were they doing here?

At once, however, his mind returned to his own situation. The back gate! Peter raced toward the stable. In the confusion, he was just one running figure among many. With a quick tug he loosened Oscar's halter rope. Not taking the time to put on a headset or saddle, he swung onto the horse's gleaming back. Outside the stable, Oscar reared in excitement and then shot forward, spurred on by his master.

Several men were just closing the back gate when the horse thundered down on them and knocked them aside. Peter shot across the little bridge and rode on into the deep shadows of the forest. Once he was well into the woods, Peter slowed down. A good rider, he knew how to control his horse merely by steering him with the pressure of his knees or prodding him with his heels.

Under cover of the thick trees he steered his horse toward the front of the castle to see what was happening. With a shock, he stopped still.

ETER urged Oscar into the shadow of a large tree and stared at the castle in astonishment. Gathered before the front gate a large group of riders milled about, brandishing torches. Their shouts were angry and threatening. But had he heard correctly? Yes, he heard it again. They were shouting his name! What did that mean?

"We want Bettelburg! Open the gate and give us Bettelburg! We want that fur thief! That sneaking rent-robber!"

Peter trembled with indignation. Where had they gotten such an idea? He hadn't stolen anyone's furs or rent. Suddenly he saw who the men at the gate were—the local farmers. He had seen many of them at the inn on the night of his arrival. They were armed now and in a dangerous mood. Had they come with pitchforks and flails to capture him? Peter didn't know what to think. What made them believe that he was behind their troubles?

Then his eyes fell on one of the riders—a slim figure with long, blond hair. A farmer carrying a torch rode right past her, and Peter started when he saw who it was. Alma! What was she doing with this mob? She didn't look like their prisoner; no one was holding her horse.

All at once another sound caught Peter's ear, a sound that rose above the shouts of the mob. Peter caught his breath, forgetting, for a moment, Alma and the farmers. The high wailing sound drowned out everything else, and then it sank slowly to a hoarse groan. There was no mistaking it: it was the same sound he had heard when he was lying in bed in Thune's attic. But then the piercing sound had come from the old mill. This time it came from the castle. He looked on with rapt attention as he saw the heavy drawbridge slowly begin to rise.

The wail increased in pitch again, almost hurting Peter's ears. In his mind he heard Thune's frightened words, "D-d-did you hear the ghost?" But now Peter knew where the sound was coming from. In the castle courtyard stood two huge wooden windlasses. A chain ran from each windlass to the drawbridge. The soldiers inside the castle were now turning the windlasses which would reel in the chains and draw up the bridge. Ungreased and unused for years, the windlasses squealed alarmingly with every rotation. This was the source of the piercing, almost human wail that arose from the castle.

As soon as he realized what was making the sound, he berated himself for his stupidity. Why hadn't he thought of it sooner? That sound of a squealing axle —that was the secret of Ravenhurst Mill. The axle of the waterwheel must have been turned! Peter also knew how it had been done. What he didn't know, however, was why.

Turning his horse with his knees, Peter rode into the

woods, threading a route through the trees. He scolded himself for not taking Oscar to the village blacksmith that afternoon, for he needed to make demands on him now despite his sore leg. He hoped that he wouldn't cause Oscar any permanent damage. The horse limped more and more as he plodded on through the snow. But soon the dark shape of the mill loomed ahead. Peter was becoming quite familiar with these woods.

Before Oscar stopped, Peter had leaped from his back. He started to run across the moonlit clearing toward the old mill, but halted abruptly. What was that in the snow? Hoofprints! They had to be new; it had snowed earlier that evening. Someone had been here recently. The hoofprints led to the mill, but there were no human footprints near the door. At the door, the hoofprints turned and led across the clearing to vanish into the woods.

The dead raven still dangled above the mill door where Peter had hung it. Peter tried to picture what had happened.

Suppose the man dressed as the countess was the black phantom. After climbing out of the moat, he must have taken a horse from the stable and left the castle. Perhaps he had come straight to the mill. Why he had done so, Peter had not yet figured out, but he was beginning to feel that he soon would know. When the man had arrived here, he had spotted the gray raven over the door. And if Peter's guess was right and the gray raven served as a warning signal to the gang members, the sight of the bird must have scared the man off. The hoofprints in the snow showed that the man had ridden off at high speed. All of this was only Peter's guess-work, but it fit.

Peter walked along the side of the mill and hopped onto a large stone jutting above the water. He wasn't sure of what he was going to do, but he went on. A vague foreboding of what he would find crept into his mind, but he shook it off to concentrate on what he was doing.

Supporting himself on the mill wall with one hand, he reached behind the waterwheel with the other. His hand found the piece of trough that he remembered seeing the last time he had been here. Shifting one foot to another rock, he grasped the trough and heaved it onto the two beams that stuck out from the mill wall. Icy water cascaded over his shoulders and down his back. One more push straightened the trough. Now the water poured down right on top of the mill wheel.

Peter waited in suspense. What if all his guesses were wrong?

Slowly the big wheel began to turn with a piercing groan that hurt Peter's ears, and yet was like music to him. From far away this would sound like the wailing of some unworldly creature or the moaning of a supernatural human being. This was the ghost that had frightened the local farmers, that caused Thune to bar his door and hide deep under his blankets.

The black phantom must have set the water wheel in motion at about midnight every night. But why?

Peter jumped back onto shore and hurried to the mill door. Would he find what he half-expected to find? He entered the dark building. On the floor before him, the broken grinding stone was slowly turning. Then Peter saw it. A large hole slowly appeared under the missing section of the stone.

Before he could get out his tinder box, however, the stone had turned farther and covered the hole again.

After waiting awhile, Peter ran outside and pulled down the loose section of the trough so that the waterwheel stopped. When he returned, the hole gaped up at him. He struck a spark from his tinder box and saw an old ladder going down. Without another thought, he lowered himself into the hole and scrambled down the ladder. When he struck up another spark, he saw a short candle propped in a niche in the wall. He lit the candle and held it up to look around. In one corner of the chamber in which he stood, there was a narrow black opening.

Peter started. From the opening came a weak voice— a woman's voice. Although he had been half expecting it, it gave him a fright.

"Is that you, you thieving coward? I'll tell you nothing! Nothing! Do you hear?"

Peter steeled himself and squeezed through the narrow opening which was little more than a crack. When he emerged on the other side, he again held the candle high. He was in a small chamber with a raised platform on one end. The platform was a bed, and on the bed lay an elderly woman. His amazed stare met the equally amazed stare of the woman.

"Who are you?" she asked in astonishment. "How did you get here?"

Peter hurried forward, scattering some rodents. "I've come to rescue you." Although he already knew the answer, he asked, "Are you the countess, Alma's grandmother?"

The old woman nodded wearily.

Hastily Peter went on: "Do you feel strong enough to walk? We must leave as quickly as we can. Strange things are happening at Ravenhurst Castle."

The countess threw back her blanket and with Peter's

help rose from the wooden bed. Although her legs were stiff, she moved quite quickly. Carefully Peter helped her through the narrow opening and up the old ladder. A few minutes later they were standing in front of the mill in the moonlit clearing.

HEN the farmers with their torches and pitchforks saw that the only answer to their demands was the raising of the drawbridge, they circled to the rear of the castle. But here too they found a drawbridge raised in front of the small gate.

Suddenly several farmers galloped to the edge of the woods where a pile of felled pine trees had been stacked. They tied the trees behind their horses and dragged them to the moat. Sliding them across the ice, they quickly constructed a makeshift bridge. Soon the mob was in front of the raised bridge and the door.

"Branches! Dead branches!" someone shouted.

They piled dry branches high against the raised wooden bridge. One young farmer tossed his torch into the pile, and flames lept upward. The angry, determined group of farmers stood back and waited for the fire to do its work. When the fire had died down, several men attacked the burnt drawbridge and door with their axes. When the door at last gave way, they stormed into the courtyard, brandishing their flails and pitchforks.

They soon lowered their weapons, however, and their shouting trailed off. Instead of encountering the fierce

133

resistance they had expected, they met no one at all. The courtyard looked abandoned. At last they spotted a small group of men standing in the shadow of the main gate. They had thrown down their weapons and surrendered without a blow.

Seeing themselves vastly outnumbered, they had decided that resistance was useless. Most of their comrades had disappeared before the alarm had been sounded. Their leader and his second in command, the man with the pointed beard, were also gone. None of the men had any idea where their leaders were. Feeling betrayed and abandoned, they had no will to fight. The farmers locked them up in one of the stables. Then they spread out in all directions to find the man they had come for—the silver-tongued outsider, the one who had come to swindle them out of their furs and grain.

Some of the men lowered the drawbridge to the front castle gate as Alma rode through the courtyard, looking around anxiously. Would the angry farmers find Peter? And if they found him, what would they do to him? Alma was afraid to think about it. Biting her lip, she looked up at the castle keep and saw the flicker of torchlight in the windows. The farmers were searching everywhere. Would they find him? Where was he hiding?

Suddenly she heard shouting. The men began running back to their horses. Mounting, they spurred their horses out the rear gate and toward the forest. Alma looked on in bafflement. She stopped one of the last ones out to ask why everyone was leaving. He shouted that somebody had found hoofprints outside the wall and along the edge of the forest.

Alma's heart rose and then fell. Apparently Peter had escaped the castle. But would the angry farmers catch him anyway? Again she bit her lip. What should she do? She was torn in two directions. She wanted to dismount and run into the castle to find her grandmother. Was she in the main hall? She must have been frightened terribly by the attack on the castle. On the other hand, Alma also wanted to follow the farmers. If she was there when they caught up with Peter, perhaps she could keep them from carrying out their worst threats. The same little demon that yesterday had whispered, "Are you sure you can trust him?" now whispered, "Are you sure he's the deceiver you think he is?"

Alma hesitated no longer. When she got back, she'd be able to see her grandmother, but now she had to save a man's life. She dug her heels into her horse's flanks and galloped out through the gate to follow the farmers. She followed the torchlights through the forest, running her horse as fast as she dared. Suddenly she saw that the leaders of the procession had stopped. They had reached a small clearing in the woods, the clearing in front of the old mill.

The farmers shuddered. The mill itself frightened them. However, in front of the mill stood something even more frightening. A black apparition stood motionless in the snow before the door.

"The ghost!" wailed one of the men.

As men began to turn their horses to flee, suddenly Alma pressed forward through the mounted riders.

"Grandma!" she cried.

With a shock of gladness she recognized the figure that had frightened the farmers so badly. She galloped into the clearing, slid off her horse, and threw her arms about her grandmother's neck.

"Grandma . . . what . . . how did you get here?"

The farmers looked on, stunned and confused. The moonlight and their own spooked fancies had convinced them that the black figure in front of the mill was the ghost everyone had been talking about. But now they saw the young woman running up to the eerie figure to embrace it. Did she call it grandma? Yes, now they saw it too. It was indeed the countess standing there in the moonlit winter night.

But how did she get here? What was she doing here so late at night and all by herself?

Out of deeply ingrained habit they removed their caps and slowly drew closer.

HAT same night Thune had been lying in bed deep under the blankets. On a low stool beside his bed a small oil lamp flickered. The black dog lay sleeping in front of the fireplace.

Thune tossed restlessly from side to side, his mind awhirl with thoughts and images. The other farmers would be sitting in front of the fire in the inn, venting their anger and despair. Thune, however, had gone to bed early. What good would it do to sit around griping?

Sometimes he drifted off into sleep, but then he would come awake again. The dog whined softly as he dreamt.

Suddenly Thune's eyes popped wide open. He pulled the blankets up to his chin and listened. A long, drawn-out wail sent chills through Thune's bones. It was the ghost of Ravenhurst Mill. Thune trembled. It wasn't midnight yet. The ghost was early tonight.

The sound died away. After listening for a while, Thune turned on his side to go to sleep, but then he got an even greater scare.

Someone was pounding on his door and shouting, "Open up! Open up! Right now!"

Thune sat up, clutching the blankets so tightly that his knuckles turned white. Who was that? What did this mean? The door shook as someone kicked it. The bolts creaked. Another kick and the door crashed open.

Thune had ducked under the blankets, but now peeked out through a little crack.

The ghost!

In the doorway stood a black apparition. It was a woman. Her face was covered by a black veil, and in her hand she held a sword. Her skirts clung to her legs as if wet. Barking wildly, the dog sprang forward, but when he was met by a heavy boot he retreated growling to a corner of the room.

Thune closed his eyes tightly, terrified to open them again. His heart nearly stopped when he felt an icy hand close on his neck. He was dragged out of bed and plunked into a chair. His wrists were tied behind him with a piece of cloth.

When at last he dared to open his eyes, Thune couldn't see the ghost. He could only hear it moving about behind his chair. When it moved toward the table and into sight, Thune's jaw dropped in astonishment. Before him stood not a ghost in a black dress but a man dressed in Thune's clothes. The pants and shirt were much too wide for him and the sleeves too short. He looked more like a scarecrow than a ghost.

The man paid no attention to Thune. He pulled a stool toward him with the toe of his boot and sat down. Then he took a piece of sausage and a chunk of bread from the table and ate greedily. Although Thune had been frightened out of his wits by the black apparition, now he was seething with anger. He yearned to get his hands on this thief who was stealing his food. But he was tied so tightly to his chair that he couldn't move.

Suddenly the stranger stopped chewing and lifted his head to listen. Thune also heard something—far away, but it was coming closer. It sounded like the clamor of hunters on the trail of a fox. The man quickly stuffed the sausage into his pocket and with a couple of long strides vanished into the darkness outside the door.

As Peter had helped the countess out of the secret hiding place beneath the mill, and they had emerged outside, his ears had caught the faint sound of approaching hoofbeats. Soon he could hear voices shouting to one another in the woods. They were still far away, but he knew what this meant. The farmers had found Oscar's tracks in the snow. Quickly he asked the countess to excuse him, apologized for having to leave her alone. He assured her that the men approaching on horseback would see to it that she was returned safely to the castle.

Swiftly he swung back onto Oscar's back and urged his limping mount into the woods and away from the sounds of hoofbeats and voices. He followed in the tracks of the earlier visitor to the mill. He couldn't ride fast because he was afraid of losing the trail. After some time Peter came to the edge of the forest. The tracks led across the field toward Thune's cabin. As he approached the cabin, he saw a dark shadow moving near the well. Slowly, cautiously Peter drew closer. A large brown horse was tied there. The tracks Peter had been following also stopped at the well.

Peter thought fast. Then he circled the house and stopped in the narrow space between the cabin and the shed. Here no one would spot Oscar. Quietly Peter crept to the nearest window. It was shuttered, but by standing on his tiptoes he could look inside through a knothole.

There, beside a pile of wet clothes, stood the man he had fought in the castle. He was just pulling on a pair of Thune's pants. Thune was sitting in a chair, his hands tied behind his back.

Peter's first impulse was to storm into the cabin and jump his enemy. But he didn't. He knew that it wouldn't be long before the farmers picked up his trail and followed it here. They were determined to have his hide. How would he defend himself against so many?

At the same time Peter had to find a way to wreck the black phantom's plan to escape with all of the furs and the grain. A plan flashed into Peter's mind. He'd have to act fast. He stole toward the horse tied up to the well. Patting the animal on the neck to calm it, he lifted one of its forelegs. He took out the raven-knife and slipped the point between the hoof and the horseshoe. He pried, but the horseshoe was well-fastened. Peter pried and wiggled some more, driving the knife in further. At last the shoe popped loose and Peter tugged it free. He hadn't hurt the horse, but now it would begin to limp just like Oscar.

Lowering the horse's foreleg, he listened closely. He thought he heard the faint noise of approaching riders. Finished just in time, he darted back into the shadows between the cabin and the shed. His ears had not fooled him; now he clearly heard the drum of approaching hooves.

The cabin door banged open and Peter retreated farther into the shadows. The black phantom, dressed in Thune's clothes, bounded outside and ran to his horse. Quickly untying it, he vaulted into the saddle and galloped off toward the swamp. He must have heard the farmers approaching too. Soon Peter saw a row of torches bobbing through the trees. When they reached the open field, the men began shouting and pointing. They had spotted the man who had just left Thune's cabin and, as Peter had hoped, immediately assumed that it was the man they were after. The posse of angry farmers thundered past the cabin and raced toward the swamp.

ETER stepped from the shadows and swiftly entered the cabin. With the raven-handled knife, he cut through the cloth that held Thune to the chair. Then he dropped the horseshoe in the big man's lap.

"Here, that's yours. It's a special horseshoe guaranteed to bring you good luck. Your friends were following the trail of a man on a limping horse and they still are, but they don't know that it's a different man and a different horse."

Pulling a sheepskin from Thune's bed, Peter draped it about the man's shoulders and pushed him out the door into the moonlit night.

"Let's go, Thune. I need your help."

Peter swung onto his horse, and before Thune realized what was happening, he felt himself being pulled up behind Peter. They were following the band of farmers. The dog ran along beside them, yapping excitedly. Peter let Oscar set his own pace. After climbing a slight rise in the terrain, he stopped.

Thune, looking over Peter's shoulder, saw the string of torchlights dancing in the distance. "Wh-what's that? What's going on?"

Peter didn't reply, for his attention was elsewhere. Beyond the riders, the river lay like a silver ribbon in the moonlight. And beyond the river, dark clouds were piling up. Peter wondered whether more snow was coming. He scanned the river, but he didn't see what he was looking for. Far away he did see the two ships that held the furs and grain he had bought.

Now he set himself a new direction. The farmers would reach the river upstream from the ships. Peter suspected that the man dressed as the countess had been signaling to his men aboard the ships, for the light that had appeared in response had come from this direction. What had the signals meant? Peter stopped his horse and dismounted in the snow.

"Listen, Thune, can you ride without a saddle and without reins?"

Thune nodded. "No problem."

"Good. The lights you asked about belong to your farmer friends from the inn."

Thune's eyebrows shot up in surprise, but Peter continued. "I can't explain now. There's no time. But I want you to ride to them and tell them to capture the man they are chasing and take him to the castle. Wait, that's not all. Tell them to lock him up in the cellar beneath the drawbridge. They'll find another dozen or so men already locked up there. Warn them not to let any of them escape. Got that?"

Peter saw that Thune didn't understand any of it, but that didn't matter.

"On your way!"

For a moment Peter watched Thune riding off, but he soon lost sight of him, for dark clouds passed in front of the moon, shrouding the countryside in darkness.

"Hush, boy, you'll be all right. You just stick with me."

Peter was holding the black dog by the collar to keep him from following Thune. Whining softly, the dog tried to pull loose. "Hush, boy! Let's go."

Peter walked toward the river's edge. The two ships lay anchored downriver about a stone's throw from the bank. As far as he could tell in the darkness, no one was standing guard aboard the ships. Taking out the raven-handled knife, he cut a long, sturdy willow branch. Then he hopped aboard one of the large ice floes slowly drifting by with the current, pulling the dog with him. Using the branch, he pushed the ice floe away from the bank. Hopping from floe to floe, he was soon drifting silently alongside one of the ships.

Peter clambered aboard and pulled the dog after him by the scruff of the neck. After standing still for several moments to make sure that he hadn't been discovered, he began to watch the dog. That afternoon a theory, actually no more than a suspicion, had formed in his mind. He had brought the dog with him for a specific purpose. The dog sniffed the air. It circled uncertainly for a moment and then moved forward, his nose to the deck. At the foredeck he pushed his nose into a pile of sacks and whined softly as he tried to dig through the sacks with his forepaws.

Peter pushed the sacks aside and moved two bales, uncovering a small, square trap door latched with an iron pin. When Peter opened the hatch, the dog almost knocked him over in his eagerness. Muffled voices sounded below. The dog stuck his head so far into the hold that he almost tumbled in, and he yelped happily.

"Castor!" A man's voice exclaimed from the darkness. Peter looked up. He had heard another sound—one that had come from behind him. Turning, he saw a shadow flitting aft. Swiftly Peter grabbed the dog and dropped through the opening. He struck a spark from his tinderbox and found just what he had expected. Groping around, he quickly cut through several ropes, hissing, "Hurry; everyone up to the deck. Hurry!"

A confused, questioning murmur arose. Peter hoisted himself back onto the deck and looked around. Sure enough, he spotted movement near the wheelhouse. "Come on; hurry!" he whispered over his shoulder. Someone was already climbing up behind him. The dog greeted the man jubilantly and licked his face. "Good boy, Castor! Take it easy!"

In a few moments eight husky men had joined Peter on the deck. They were the soldiers from the castle who had been replaced by the strangers. Yes, that wagon had been carrying more than a load of branches. And the dog he had met at Thune's cabin had been the same dog that had escaped from the castle late at night when Peter had opened the rear gate. Putting things together, Peter had begun to suspect that the countess's former soldiers were being kept prisoner somewhere near the river. And what better place than on the ships? But without the sharp nose of a dog looking for his master, he never would have found them. Peter pointed to the shadow on the aft deck and whispered, "Let's go!"

The men understood Peter at once. Although they didn't know him, he had freed them and they accepted his leadership. Spreading out, they advanced swiftly. When they reached the rear deck, the door to the crew's quarters suddenly slammed shut. The soldiers quickly kicked it open, however, and Peter discovered Dandy Dan, the lackey with the pointed beard, hiding in one corner. This time he wasn't wearing his mocking little grin. Instead, his eyes were filled with fear.

Two men grabbed him, one by each shoulder, and yanked him to his feet. Peter stood before him and demanded, "Where's my money?"

"Money? What money?" the man blustered.

"The money I paid for the grain and furs that you stole."

One of the soldiers searched Dandy Dan's person and found a heavy purse filled with coins. Peter weighed it in his hand and reckoned that the entire amount was still there.

"Lock him up," he ordered. "We'll question him some more later."

From outside came the sound of taunting laughter. Peter ran onto the deck and saw a black shape behind the ship. Again he heard laughter; someone seemed to think something was very funny. The black shape, which was disappearing farther into the night, seemed to be a raft manned by four or five men. Strange, it looked as if it were floating upstream!

But that was impossible. Then, with a sudden shock, Peter realized what was happening. The raft wasn't floating upstream. It was standing still. The ship was drifting downstream. The bandits on the boat must have noticed that they had been boarded and they had quietly lowered themselves over the side onto the raft. Then they had disconnected the anchor chain, to which they had anchored the raft. Only Dandy Dan hadn't had time to escape.

What now? Now both ships were drifting helplessly downstream. The soldiers knew nothing about sailing.

Peter peered across the water and the fields. An idea took shape in his mind. Hadn't he seen a tar barrel standing along the railing? Yes, there it was. Quickly he tested the wind.

"Two of you men give me a hand with this barrel. We'll bring it to the rear deck."

Peter took out his tinder box. It took several attempts but finally the tar caught fire, and the flames of a giant torch leaped high into the night sky.

For a long time the ships drifted with the sluggish current, the tar barrel blazing fruitlessly. Peter paced up and down the deck, constantly staring downriver. He saw nothing but darkness, however, and he heard nothing but the gentle scrape of ice floes along the side of the ship.

Suddenly he stopped and stared hard at one spot. Far away a tiny point of light twinkled in the darkness. Was that what he had been looking for? Yes, the light was coming closer, and he heard voices shouting. Soon the rigging of another ship loomed up in the darkness, and the ship slowly drew alongside. Ropes with grappling hooks were tossed over the railings. Men ran back and forth. Peter climbed onto the rail and jumped across to the other ship. In the light of the blazing tar barrel he had recognized someone aboard the other ship—his father!

The letter Thune had delivered had arrived in time to do some good. Peter was extremely glad he had written when he did. Soon after his arrival at Ravenhurst Castle he had begun to suspect that there would be trouble. When suspicion turned to certainty, he had asked his father to come in case he needed help. He had known that his father was doing business with one of his own ships at a city at the mouth of the river. According to

Peter's calculations, if his letter had been delivered in time, his father should have been on his way upriver. Peter's calculations had proven right.

His father's ship had been anchored for the night when a watch had spotted the burning tar barrel. Now the sailors of his father's ship divided themselves among the three ships and turned them upstream. Peter hated to think what would have happened had he drifted out to sea with the soldiers.

A T FIRST light, the ships had returned to the place where they had been anchored. By the time the sun began to rise, the men were at the castle.

Peter went to check the prisoners held in the cellar room where he himself had been trapped. The gang was all there, except for two. Last night the band of farmers had captured the sailors on the raft when they had landed. But their leader, the black phantom, had escaped. The farmers had pursued him to the river, where he had waded out into the icy water and climbed onto an ice floe. The ice floe had been swept into the middle of the river.

When Peter heard the story, he clenched his fists in frustration. He had wanted to see the man who had thrown the raven-knife at him locked up. But it was no use crying over spilt milk. Perhaps the man would have been better off being hauled before a judge than floating downriver in wet clothes and without food on a night like last night. Would he be able to paddle to shore somewhere? Or would he be carried all the way down the river into the wide, gray sea? Peter shuddered. What an end!

The other man who had vanished without a trace was Turnip-nose. The last time Peter had seen him had been under the drawbridge, after he had flattened him with a punch to the jaw. Was he still lying there? Peter went outside and swung to the ledge beside the moat. He couldn't help laughing. The man was gone, but under the bridge lay a rotten tooth. Peter's fist had done a good job. After regaining his senses, the man must have seized the chance to leave the castle unseen. Peter didn't mind. He hadn't been such a bad fellow—just stupid. Now he was no doubt plodding through the woods, cured of his toothache.

Peter climbed back onto the drawbridge, turning toward the castle, but then in the courtyard he spotted a soldier with a black dog at his heels. He was wearing a tall boot on one foot and a clog on the other. Peter called him and told him to go along with Thune. He'd find his other boot in Thune's cabin. The man stared at him disbelievingly. How could his boot possibly have ended up at Thune's place? Peter laughed at the man's incredulous stare. "Thune will explain. I'd like you to do one other thing. You and Thune go on to the old mill after you've picked up your boot. Under the millstone you'll find a bed. It belongs to the innkeeper. I'd appreciate it if you'd return it to him."

The countess and Alma were sitting in the main hall before the fireplace, where a huge fire crackled. Peter's father was sitting with them. All traces of last night's fight were gone except for the broken window, which had been covered by a thick tapestry.

When Peter entered the room, a deep flush spread over Alma's face. How had she ever doubted Peter's loyalty? He had risked his life for her and her grandma!

Red with shame, she confessed how she had doubted him and had told the farmers that he was the ringleader of the thieves.

Peter laughed aloud when she told them how she had overheard his conversation with Turnip-nose. "I don't blame you for doubting me after that," he said. "But that's all behind us. Let's not even talk about it anymore. Except one thing still puzzles me," said Peter, turning to the countess. "How did all this begin, and how did you end up a prisoner in the old mill?"

The old woman smiled sadly behind her veil. In spite of himself Peter felt admiration for the skillful way the ringleader had played the role of the countess. His veil had been a little thicker so that Peter had seen nothing of his face, and he had used a different cane—a sword cane. But his voice and gestures had fooled Peter completely.

The countess told them that some time ago a distant relative and his friend had visited the castle. She had not even recognized the cousin at first, because she had met him only once before and then he had been a boy. Although she had heard rumors that he had turned bad when he grew up, and although she had taken a keen dislike to his friend, the man with the pointed beard, she had invited them to stay for a few days. One day they had forced her to go with them down to her carriage. She had planned to call out to her soldiers as she was taken through the courtyard, but when she came outside, the courtyard was occupied by a band of strange, rough-looking soldiers. The castle had been seized by a gang of robbers.

She had been taken to the old mill and had been well-provided for. Every night about midnight her cousin had come to bring her food and drink. When they left with the year's profits, he had told her, she would be returned to the castle unharmed.

Although Peter realized that talking about her experiences was probably unpleasant for the elderly woman, he was still bothered by one question. His father, however, was ahead of him. "How did the man know about that hideout under the mill? And who built it?" he asked.

Then the countess told them about her mad great-grandfather, the hermit count. She described his strange fears and his death on the waterwheel. Years ago, when as a boy her distant relative had visited the castle, he had spent much time exploring the woods. On one of his outings he must have discovered the secret place where the mad count had hoped to hide from his imaginary enemies. No doubt the old count had been killed as he tried to turn the waterwheel to open the entrance to his underground chamber.

NE evening two weeks later the farmers were once again gathered around the fireplace in the inn. Everyone was talking, and the topic of conversation was everyone's favorite. They talked about the siege of the castle by torchlight, and about the search for Master Peter, whom they had mistaken for the ringleader of the thieves, and about the ghost of Ravenhurst Mill, which had turned out not to be a ghost at all.

Suddenly the door burst open and a cloud of fine snow blew inside as it had that night when the countess's granddaughter had appeared in the doorway. This time, however, it was big Thune who entered. His eyes sparkled with delight.

Slamming the door behind him, he cried, "Listen, men, I've just had a visit from Master Peter. He and his father are still guests at the castle. He asked me to invite you all to the castle the day after tomorrow. That's right—everyone! There's going to be a big celebration. Guess why . . . That's right, there's going to be a wedding!"

"Hurrah! Three cheers for Master Peter! Three cheers for Miss Alma!"

155

Thune held up his hands. "Quiet! That's not all. They want us to help celebrate and—"

"Hurrah!"

"Let me finish! There's more. When we come for the wedding, the countess will return everything that the thieves collected unfairly."

"Hurrah! Three cheers for the countess!"

High above the castle roof flew a lonely raven, cawing harshly. It wheeled around the towers and scanned the courtyard with its sharp, beady eyes, looking for its master. Finding no trace of him, it flapped toward the forest. There it glided down to a clearing surrounded by a dense stand of trees. Stepping high, it strutted toward the old mill and cocked its head to look at the old building. On a bent nail over the doorway hung a dead raven—a gray one.

The black raven on the ground stretched its neck. Then it cocked its head to the other side and blinked its black eyes. "Caw, caw!"

Beating the air with its large wings, it rose above the treetops and flew off. Over the swamp it spotted a flight of ravens and joined them, flying across the vast, gray landscape into the gray distance.